R0082639550

06/2014

Alexis
the icing
on the
cupcake

This book is a work of fiction. Any references to historical events, real people, or real places are used fictitiously. Other names, characters, places, and events are products of the author's imagination, and any resemblance to actual events or places or persons, living or dead, is entirely coincidental.

SIMON SPOTLIGHT

An imprint of Simon & Schuster Children's Publishing Division

1230 Avenue of the Americas, New York, New York 10020

Copyright © 2014 by Simon & Schuster, Inc.

All rights reserved, including the right of reproduction in whole or in part in any form.

SIMON SPOTLIGHT and colophon are registered trademarks of Simon & Schuster, Inc.

Text by Elizabeth Doyle Carey

Chapter header illustrations by Maryam Choudhury

Designed by Laura Roode

For information about special discounts for bulk purchases, please contact Simon & Schuster Special Sales at 1-866-506-1949 or business@simonandschuster.com.

Manufactured in the United States of America 0514 FFG

First Edition 2 4 6 8 10 9 7 5 3 1

ISBN 978-1-4814-0468-6 (pbk)

ISBN 978-1-4814-0469-3 (hc)

ISBN 978-1-4814-0470-9 (eBook)

Library of Congress Control Number 2014935801

CUPCAKE DIARIES

Alexis
the icing
on the
cupcake

by coco simon

Simon Spotlight
New York   London   Toronto   Sydney   New Delhi

CHAPTER 1

Growth Spurt

My ankles were freezing.

It was a cold and rainy morning, even though it was almost Memorial Day, and the weather was a little fluky: hot and muggy one day, chilly and cool the next. So maybe that explained my cold ankles. But the rest of me wasn't chilly. My ankles felt . . . bare, despite the fact I had on long pants. I stretched out my foot at the breakfast table and looked down. Wait, why was there suddenly so much ankle showing from the bottom of my pant leg? These pants weren't capris! Had they shrunk?

I stood up and shimmied the pants down a little so that they covered more of my ankles. My older sister, Dylan, gave me a glance over her teapot and then looked back at what she was reading. Now my ankles were covered, but my pants were riding too low for comfort. They were practically falling off my hips, actually.

"Argh!" I cried in frustration.

"What's the matter, Lexi?" asked Dylan in a slightly annoyed tone. "I'm trying to have a peaceful morning here." Dylan's been trying to be all mature these days, drinking tea and acting really patient and calm no matter what the situation. She took this relaxation and meditation class, and now she goes around telling us that the house has to be her "Zen place."

"My pants don't fit!" I cried very un-Zenlike. "And they're not that old! I just bought them with Grandma over spring break!"

Dylan rolled her eyes. "You must've shrunk them. You're supposed to line dry cotton pants like that."

"I do!" I protested. "Always!"

Dylan thought for a minute, then she sighed and shook her head. "Then it could only be one thing," she said, returning to the fascinating back of the cereal box.

I guess she wasn't going to tell me unless I asked. And I really, *really* didn't want to ask. But the suspense was killing me.

"What?"

Dylan sighed again, as if it was all so obvious and I was such a nitwit. "Hello? Growth spurt!"

"What?"

"You grew! Happens all the time. That's why they call it 'growing up.'" She shook her head.

"But that *fast*?"

She nodded. "It can happen overnight sometimes. You come down in the morning and suddenly you can see things on the top shelf of the fridge that you'd swear you couldn't see when you went to bed the night before."

"Really?" I walked over to the fridge and opened it. I glanced around the top shelf: yogurt, pickles, mustard . . . Wait, had that temperature dial always been back there? I knew I'd never seen it before because I would have had some fun tweaking it to see if different temperatures saved us money or made things icy. Had the fridge really come like that? I didn't dare ask Dylan.

Feeling slightly freaked out, I shut the door and stood with my back to it, hands still on the handle.

There was no doubt about it.

I had grown.

"So what should I do?" I asked Dylan.

"About what?"

I gestured helplessly at my naked ankles.

Dylan stood up to wash her cup in the sink. "Buy new pants," she said.

Before I could go to school, I had to change my pants, but I had to try on two other pairs before I found one that fit. At school I ran into my best friend, Emma Taylor, on the way to my locker.

"I grew," I said, falling into step beside her.

"I know," she agreed.

I stopped dead in my tracks. "Wait! *Really?* You could tell?"

Emma stopped too and nodded. "Uh-huh. I have to look up at you more when I talk to you now."

"Well, when were you going to tell me?"

Emma laughed and started walking again. "Seriously, Lexi? You need me to *tell* you that you grew?"

"I don't know. I mean, it's not like I noticed it myself." I unlocked my locker and was startled to see how packed my top shelf was. "Ugh. This locker is a pit. I need to clean this thing out!"

Emma laughed again. "See? Suddenly, you can see stuff that's high up. Maybe you could check the top shelf in my locker and see if my mouth guard for soccer is up there."

I laughed. "What, now I'm renting out my height?"

She giggled. "You could!"

"What, for locker cleanouts?"

"Yeah, you could charge. . . ."

My money-making senses tingled a little. I do have a head for business. Could I earn cash by cleaning out lockers? Probably. The bigger question is, would I want to? A thought for another day.

Speaking of money . . . "Hey, are we meeting today?" I asked. Our Cupcake Club usually meets on Fridays at lunch to plan out upcoming jobs and experiment with new recipes, as well as bake for our regular customers and any weekend jobs we might have lined up. Plus, we always get together at Friday lunch and bring cupcakes; it's a delicious tradition.

"Yup," said Emma. "We have our lunch meeting, obviously, and then after school we're on for baking. Mia can come now that she'll be at her mom's this weekend. Let's do it at my house."

"Great. I brought the ledger and everything, just in case we were able to meet. I'll see you later in the cafeteria," I said, and we headed off to our classes. Down the hall, I stopped for a quick gulp of water at the fountain.

I swear, I've never noticed how low that thing is. It's, like, elementary school–size! They should really have it raised.

"Lexxxiiiiii!" called Mia from our table in the corner. I cringed a little and glanced around to see if anyone else had heard her call me that. It's not that I really mind if my family or my very closest friends call me "Lexi" in private. It's just that lately it has been rubbing me the wrong way. It sounds babyish, and I don't want it to spread. And also, just secretly, it does bug me a teeny, tiny bit when Mia and Katie call me "Lexi" because it's really my childhood nickname from before I knew them. Like, they don't really have the right to call me that. But whatever.

I crossed the lunchroom with my tray and went to sit beside Mia.

"What's up?" asked Mia. "Cute pants. Haven't seen those before."

Mia is a major fashionista (her mom is a professional stylist) so I always pay close attention to her fashion advice.

"Seriously? Do you like these pants?" I asked, looking down. "I've had them for a while, but they were always too big. Now they fit. They cover my ankles, anyway." I shrugged.

"Definitely cute. My faves are your pale pink ones, though."

I sighed and picked up a forkful of chili. "They shrank. Or, actually, I grew. They don't fit anymore already!"

"Can't you get them shortened a little more and wear them as capris?" she asked. "They'd be cute with a white sleeveless blouse."

I chewed my chili and thought about it. "Maybe. The thing is . . . I don't look so good in cropped pants."

"Oh, come on! With those long, thin legs of yours, you'd look good in anything," said Mia.

I couldn't help but smile a little, since a compliment from Mia means a lot. "Thanks. I'm not sure that's true, but whatever."

"Oh please, I'd kill to be tall and thin like you." At that point in the conversation, Emma and Katie joined us. I did feel a little better after what Mia said about my figure, even though I was still frustrated about my wardrobe.

"Hey, listen, we got a good order over the weekend from my neighbor," said Katie. "Remember Mrs. Dreher who had the baby shower? She's having a summer kick-off barbecue slash pool party next Sunday, and she wants us to bake six dozen 'beachy' cupcakes for her."

"Great!" I said. "Did you quote her a price or should I follow up?"

Katie smiled. "I gave her a ballpark price and said our CFO would follow up with an e-mail once we knew for sure what we were baking."

"Excellent." I nodded happily. I love it when our business runs like a well-oiled machine.

Mia started brainstorming. "Remember those cool pool cupcakes we did for the swim team fundraiser? Maybe we should do those again?"

"Oh, but remember how the frosting melted on those when it got hot in the indoor pool area?" reminded Emma. "We wouldn't want that to happen if it's a hot day for the barbecue."

I groaned at the memory. That swim team episode had almost been a major catastrophe. We'd almost ended up *losing* money, which is something I hate!

"Let's do something with light brown sugar around the edges—like fake sand?" suggested Katie.

"Ooh, that's good!" agreed Mia.

Emma's eyes sparkled suddenly. "I think we need a field trip!" she said. "Let's go to the beach!"

"Yes!" exclaimed Mia. "When?"

Emma shrugged and looked around at all of us. "This weekend?"

I thought about my schedule. We have exams next week, and I have a big paper due. Of course, I've been studying, so I'm in pretty good shape for the tests. And I'm more than halfway done with the paper. Plus, I have the rest of it mapped out. I knew Mom and Dad would be okay with the plan. "I'm up for it!" I said.

Everyone agreed. We'd go tomorrow, providing all the parents said it was okay, and we'd still have Sunday for homework.

"Yay!" said Katie, clapping her hands. "I can wear my new swimsuit!"

Hmm. Mentally, I scanned my closet to think about what I'd wear. I guess I wouldn't know until I went home and tried things on. I was not looking forward to it.

CHAPTER 2

Alexis, Not Lexi

*A*fter school, we had our usual Friday baking session, making our standard weekly order for our number-one customer, Mona at The Special Day bridal salon. Hanging out in Emma's kitchen between batches, I kept hoping her brother Matt, the crush of my life, would appear. But after looking expectantly at the door for maybe the fifth time, Emma finally busted me and said, "Lexi, he's at an away lacrosse game today. He won't be home until really late."

I could feel myself blushing beet red. "Sorry," I mumbled.

Emma laughed. Most of the time, she was a good sport about my crush. "Sorry to disappoint you."

Her other brother Sam showed up a little while after that, just as I was bending over to take two trays of mini cupcakes out of the oven. I stood up and placed the trays on the counter to cool, and as I did, Sam said, "Whoa, Lexi! You grew!"

I have known Sam all my life, and though he is great-looking, I have never had a crush on him (unlike Katie and Mia!).

I stood up straight. "You think?"

He nodded. "Big time. You're all the way up to my shoulder now." (Sam is really tall.)

"Huh," I said. "I hope I don't keep going."

"Nah, tall girls are cool."

"I guess . . . ," I said. *As long as the boys are tall too,* I added silently. I wondered now if I might be taller than Matt. I racked my brain to think of when was the last time I saw him. And were we both standing? Matt is not as tall as Sam; I don't even know if he'll be a tall guy one day. I would hate it if I were taller than him. It might sound silly and old-fashioned, but I just like for the guy to be the taller one in a couple. Not that *we're* a couple. Or that we ever will be. Aaaaargh!

Sam left the kitchen, and Mia and Katie swooned, clutching their hands to their hearts. "How can you be so calm around him, Alexis?" asked Mia.

"I know! And he just told you you're cool, too!" said Katie.

"I don't have a crush on him." I laughed. Then I joked, "Seriously, guys, get a grip. He's my best friend's older brother. He's known me forever. . . ."

Emma smirked at me, and the other girls laughed as they got the Matt reference.

Trying to be all casual, I said, "Hey, Emma, has . . . uh . . . Matt grown lately?" I busied myself stirring some white frosting, so I didn't have to look at her expression.

"Don't worry, Alexis. I'm sure he's still bigger than you."

"Wait, am I *big*?" I said, whirling around. As I whirled, I knocked the aluminum bowl of frosting onto the floor. It landed, mercifully, right-side up, but with a huge clatter. A large dollop of frosting splattered out of the bowl and began oozing down the Taylors' kitchen cabinet. "Oh!" I cried.

I bent down to pick up the bowl. "Don't worry. I didn't lose much. . . ."

The others were at my side in a flash.

"Phew!" said Katie.

"Nice landing," agreed Emma.

Mia handed me a wet paper towel to wipe up the ooze.

"Thanks. That was close. Sorry to be such a klutz. But seriously"—I stood up—"*Am* I big? Like a *'big girl'*?"

Mia looked at me with a puzzled look on her face. "What does that mean?"

"I know what you're talking about," said Katie, totally getting it. "And the answer is no. That's for girls who are big and broad, like quarterbacks. You're just tall." She shrugged.

"Like, tall for my age or a freak of nature who's going to tower over people all my life?" I said miserably.

Emma came over and wrapped her arm around me. "Lexi, you're a little ahead of the curve for now, height-wise, but you're slender and graceful. . . ."

"Except for when I'm being a klutz!" I said grimly.

"And Matt is always going to be taller than you. He takes after my grandpa, who's six foot three!"

That made me feel a little better, but not much. "Well . . ." And then, I don't know why I said it, I just threw it in. "Also, I don't want to be called Lexi anymore!"

Emma looked taken aback, but she recovered quickly. "Really?" she asked.

I nodded.

"Why?" asked Mia, puzzled.

"It's babyish." I sniffed.

"I think it's the opposite!" said Katie. "I think it's sophisticated!"

"*Not!*" I cried. "It's what everyone has been calling me since I was a baby. I'm sorry to be a pain, and I will change the topic after this, but . . . do you guys mind? Since you're all my besties, if you always call me Alexis, so will everyone else. Okay?"

Mia shrugged. "Okay. I usually call you Alexis anyway."

"Sure. Whatever you want," agreed Katie, but she looked unsure as she said it.

Emma just smiled. "Me too? I love nicknames! What about 'Lex'?"

"'Lex' sounds like a guy, which is even worse for someone like me, who's as tall as a guy!"

"Oh, Le—Alexis," corrected Emma. "You're being silly now."

"All right. Well, enough about me. What do you think of my hair?" I joked.

"Hey, let's look at beach cupcake designs online!" suggested Katie.

So we gathered around the Taylors' family computer and googled design ideas, and as we finished up Mona's cupcakes, we brainstormed about what

14

to make for the barbecue and then, of course, what to wear to the beach tomorrow.

"OMG! Here we go again!" I yelled, throwing yet another article of clothing on my floor after dinner.

My mom appeared in the doorway. "Sweetheart, may I help you?" she asked. Mom doesn't like yelling. She likes to "diffuse" the situation, as she says. She learned that at one of the parenting workshops she and my dad are always going to.

I wanted to bite her head off, but I refrained because she was just being nice and because I didn't want another lecture about how yelling isn't productive. "None of my clothes fit," I said through tightly gritted teeth.

"Hmm," said my mom, biting her lip thoughtfully. "What about the new spring things you bought with Grandma?" she asked brightly.

"Too small," I said darkly.

"What? *Already?*" My mom gasped.

"Don't rub it in," I said.

My mom smiled. "That *is* frustrating. So, of course nothing from last summer fits either, then?"

"Right," I said.

"Maybe Dylan . . ."

"Ha! As if!" I said.

15

"Yeah," my mom agreed. We both knew the likelihood of Dylan lending me anything was slim to none.

My mom was quiet for a second, and then she said, "Well, Alexis, you know there are more important things in life than how you look. Hard work and kindness—"

"Mom!" I interrupted her. "I can't fit into any of my clothes! I'm not being a brat and asking for a new outfit! This is . . . potential nudity!"

My mom giggled. "Sorry, I know. Don't get mad. I was just trying to say the right thing."

"Well, don't say anything, please," I grumped.

We sat for a few seconds in silence.

Suddenly, I noticed my mom squinting at me. "You know . . . ," she singsonged. Then she turned on her heel, and before I could protest, she was down the hall and into her room like a flash.

Ugh. I knew where she was going. Now I was going to have to sit here and look through her mom clothes and be totally bummed out at how dorky they were and what a loser I was for potentially having to wear them, all the while acting appreciative and gracious, so I didn't hurt her feelings. I know I sound so spoiled right now, but I am just. So. Frustrated.

It was so rookie of me to be unprepared for this growth spurt. One of my mottoes, after all, is failing to plan is planning to fail. And I do have some money socked away for a rainy day. I was planning on using it for a nicer computer one day, but maybe I will just have to dig into it and buy some new clothes that fit.

"Here we go!" my mom singsonged again as she returned with an armload of clothes. Right away I recognized one or two things that there was *no way* I'd be caught dead in. I literally bit my tongue (not hard) to avoid saying anything mean. I took some calming breaths and counted to ten. (My mom learned that in a parenting class and always does it when she's about to lose her cool.)

"Thanks, Mom!" I said, maybe a little too cheerily because she glanced at me suspiciously. I kept a smile plastered on my face because one of Dylan's relaxation books says you can trick your brain into thinking it's happy by smiling, even when you're not happy.

Gingerly, as if they held plague-causing germs, I lifted and sifted through her clothes.

"Oh, now these shorts are really cute," she said, lifting up a pair of long pink shorts that I would never wear in a million years.

"Yeah!" I said halfheartedly. It wouldn't do to encourage her too much, especially this early on.

"What about these?" suggested my mom, holding up a pair of scalloped white shorts that were almost cute, but still a little too momish for me.

"Uuhnn." I made a pleasant, noncommittal, not-encouraging-but-not-rude sound. There was one cute turquoise T-shirt from Big Blue that I set aside, and my mom beamed. I'd always had my eye on that, and now would be the time to make my move. T-shirts aren't old ladyish, anyway.

I looked through a couple of other things and then pulled out a pair of white capris I hadn't seen before. They still had the tags on them.

"Oh, sorry. These are brand-new," I said, laying them back down.

"No, go ahead, honey. Try them on. I bought them on impulse. I'm not sure they even look good on me. I'd be happy to have you wear them."

"Thanks, Mom. That is *so* nice, but I don't need to." Now I felt bad.

"Alexis, I insist!" she pressed.

"Well . . ." They were really cute. I yanked off my pj bottoms and pulled on the capris. They weren't too high-waisted, and they had cute side-seamed pockets and a slit at the end of each leg. They were pretty comfy, actually.

"They have stretch in the fabric!" crowed my mom, like stretch had just been invented.

"Great!" I said. I went down the hall to look in the full-length mirror in her room, and as I passed Dylan's room, I made a point not in to look to see what Dylan was doing. But I heard her right behind me as I entered my parents' room.

In an enthusiastic but slightly accusatory voice, Dylan said, "Hey, where'd you get those—" There was a pause, and then she said, "Pants?"

Right then, I looked in the mirror and gasped. My legs stuck awkwardly out from the bottoms, and the hem hit me at just the wrong part of my lower leg. It wasn't clear if they were Bermuda shorts that were way too long or pants that were way too short. "I look like a scarecrow!" I cried, pulling off the pants immediately. "See! *This* is why I never wear capris!"

My mom came rushing in. "Wait! I didn't even get a good final look! I thought they were great in your room!"

Angrily, I folded the capris in half and smoothed them down, then I stomped out of the room, calling, "Mom, thank you so much. I'm not mad at you. I'm just cranky with my body!" And then I slammed my door, gently and neatly moved my mom's clothes to my chair, climbed under my covers, and turned off my light. My knees ached for some reason, and I was so frustrated, I didn't think I'd be able to get to sleep for hours, but it must've been only minutes because the next thing I knew, I was waking up and it was morning.

When I got out of bed a few moments later, I stepped on a piece of paper that was just a few inches away from my door. I bent down to read it and gasped at what it said. "Wake me up when you are ready to get dressed for the beach. I will help you. D."

"I wonder how much Mom paid her. . . ." I muttered as I went to brush my teeth, shaking my head in wonderment at Dylan's unusual kindness.

CHAPTER 3

Boys Are People Too

$\mathcal{A}$s chilly and damp as it had been yesterday, today was warm and dry: a perfect beach day!

I carefully woke Dylan up at about nine thirty, since Katie's mom was picking us up at ten thirty. I'd need at least an hour to navigate my fashion intervention by Dylan. Dylan was surprisingly pleasant upon waking up, and after a granola bar and a quick cup of tea, she was back upstairs and whipping open her shades, making her bed, and then turning to size me up.

"Now, you want to wear the turquoise T-shirt of Mom's, right?" she said with a gleam in her eye.

I nodded cautiously. "Yeeeess . . ."

Dylan nodded. "Good. So we have a nugget to start with."

Suddenly, I relaxed, realizing that this was one of those extreme makeover projects Dylan so enjoys. It would be smooth sailing after all. Dylan loves a good creative outlet every now and then, and I am usually lucky when I end up on the receiving end.

She nodded and began flicking through hangers in her closet, one efficient click after another as she evaluated and then discarded choices. A couple of times she selected something, which she hung on the doorknob, but because of my angle in the room, I couldn't see what they were.

Then she went to her dresser, flinging open the bottom drawer, where she keeps her pants in the winter and shorts in the summer. (Like me, Dylan is pretty organized.)

She grabbed two or three things, then she grabbed the hangers and gestured that I should ditch my pj bottoms and begin trying things on as she laid them on the bed.

First, I tried on supershort cut-off jeans of hers that I have always loved and my mom rarely allows her to wear.

I pulled them on, and they fit perfectly around my waist, maybe a tad loose. I looked down—not as short on me as on Dylan, but still pretty short.

"Cool! First try!" I said. But Dylan was shaking her head.

"A little . . . inappropriate," she said. "Next!"

"Wait, what?" How had that happened so fast? "But that's what Mom always says when you wear them! On me?"

Dylan shook her head again. "Now I can see what Mom means. Next!"

Sighing heavily, I took off the denim shorts. This new maturity of Dylan's was superannoying, but I couldn't exactly fight it now when it was helping me. Next, I tried on a floral-print romper. "Yuck! Really?" I asked.

Dylan sighed. "They don't work on me, either. Rompers were supposed to be the next big thing. They never took off. Next!"

I couldn't get that romper off fast enough. Eyeing the denim shorts wistfully, I pulled on a white denim miniskirt and buttoned it. It was comfy and light and looked good with the turquoise T-shirt.

I jammed my hands in the front pockets and twirled. "Well?" I asked.

Dylan was nodding silently. She looked at me from afar and then from behind. "Yup. That's it."

"Can I go look in Mom and Dad's room?" I asked.

23

"Go for it," said Dylan.

I trotted down the hall and looked in my mom's mirror. The denim skirt looked nice, and the turquoise was good with my coloring. I felt happy with what I had on for the first time in days.

"Thanks, Dilly!" I called as I skipped back down the hall.

"Anytime!" she said cheerily, which was kind of hilarious since it was a total lie. Dylan would not help me "anytime," but I was grateful for *this* time.

"Do you need help cleaning up?" I asked, standing in her doorway.

"No." She eyed me carefully. "Don't forget to put on some sunscreen. Those legs are looking neon white." Regular Dylan was back, and I was relieved.

I looked down. "Right," I agreed.

In my room, I grabbed last summer's racer-back swimsuit, which suddenly looked frayed and babyish. As I put it on under my new outfit, I made a mental note to ask my mom to get me something new. Then I grabbed a Sudoku book, my cool heart-shape red sunglasses, my wallet, and from the linen closet in the hall, a beach towel. I packed everything into a tote bag from some conference my mom had gone to for work, then jammed on a pair of flip-flops. On my way downstairs, I took a tube of sunscreen from the bathroom. Down in the kitchen, I put the sunscreen on the counter and filled a steel water bottle with cold water from the fridge, then I made myself an almond-butter sandwich on whole grain bread (my mom is a health nut) as a snack. I had a little time left before Katie was coming to get me, so I flipped on the TV in the den to watch some of my favorite show, *Celebrity Ballroom*.

I guess time got away from me because the next thing I knew, Katie was in my kitchen calling, "Helloooo!"

"OMG!" I jumped up. "Coming!" I called back. I looked at the cable box: 10:26. Katie was early. But still. I hate being late or fumbling and rushing.

In the kitchen I squealed with excitement when I saw Katie in her bikini top and gym shorts. "All ready for the beach!" I cried.

Katie was looking at me, puzzled. "Why are you all dressed up?" she asked. "I mean, you look adorable, but do you have somewhere to go after?"

My bubble was burst. I looked down at my outfit in dismay. "Wait. Is this too dressy?"

"Oh. No. Just . . . You look cute!" said Katie brightly.

Suddenly, I realized my outfit was all wrong.

And after all that work! I should have known Dylan would get all dressed up for the beach. She wears cute outfits to go to the grocery store with Mom! I looked at the clock again. Did I have time to change?

"Let's go!" said Katie.

I guess not.

Slowly, I gathered up my bag and my water bottle, and then I spotted the sunscreen on the counter. I had forgotten to put it on. Boy, I was really scatterbrained these days! It was so unlike me! I dropped the sunscreen into my bag and trudged out to the Browns' car, not as excited as I had been a little while ago. And as we picked up Emma and Mia, and I saw them in their beachy outfits (Emma in an old cotton cover-up and Mia in a sarong and a tank top), I felt even more out of sorts. Everyone admired my outfit, but they each had a look of confusion when they first saw it. Glumly, I stared out the window. I felt betrayed by my body.

Everyone was chattering and didn't seem to notice that I was quiet. Then Emma said, "Lexi—I mean, *Alexis*—guess what? Matt's going to be there today, and so will George Martinez!" She nudged Katie, since Katie has a crush on George, and even better, he has a crush on her, too! I was glad Emma had made the effort to refrain from calling me "Lexi."

Katie whooped and reached out her hand for a high five. I had to crack a smile and high-five her back.

"Is that why you got dressed up?" asked Mia from the front seat. "Did you already know?"

She wasn't trying to be mean, but I was so fed up. "I'm not that dressed up!" I cried. "It's just a T-shirt and a denim skirt! It's all I had that fit, and it's not even mine!" I took a deep breath and stared out the window.

The car was quiet for a moment, and Mrs. Brown said, "Alexis, you look lovely. Like a California beach girl! Totally natural and pretty."

I didn't even need to look at my friends to know that they were exchanging looks about me. I sighed and thanked Mrs. Brown politely.

We reached the beach and pulled out all the gear from the back of the Browns' car: beach chairs, an umbrella, a raft. It was already getting hot, even though it wasn't even noon, and I thought again of the sunscreen I hadn't yet put on.

Mrs. Brown went to park the car. She'd set up her gear on the other side of the beach from us, in case we needed her, but so she wasn't "breathing down our necks," as she put it. She cautioned us to have a buddy system for swimming and to stay in front of the lifeguard the whole time. Then she reminded us about sunscreen.

"Reapply every two hours and when you get out of the water," she said.

"I've got mine!" I said. "Anyone can borrow some. I'll put it on when we get set up."

Mrs. Brown smiled at me and said, "You are always so organized, Alexis. I love it. I know I can count on you. Make sure the other girls put some on too, okay?"

"Aye, aye, Captain," I said with a salute. I love Mrs. Brown. She's always so nice to me.

Lugging my share of the gear, I followed Emma toward the lifeguard stand. The beach was only medium-crowded, so we had our pick of some good spots. She chose a spot to the right of the stand, close to the water, where no one would get between us and the edge of the ocean, and we set up camp.

I have to admit, as soon as I peeled off my unfortunate outfit, I felt a little better. My swimsuit was a tad small, and I had to keep pulling it down for decency's sake, but since I was planning on spending most of my day in the water, it would be okay.

"Hey! There are the boys!" called Katie. She began waving at Matt and George and some other guys who were walking toward us along the water's edge.

Ugh. I didn't want them to have an instant full view of me in my too-small bathing suit, so I took off into the water, crashing awkwardly through the white foam and belly flopping into a wave that promptly smacked me and rolled me under.

When I stood up, gasping and wiping sand off my face a moment later, I was face-to-face with Matt Taylor—love of my life, total god—who looked adorable in a pair of colorful surf trunks and a navy blue T-shirt that showed off the muscles in his arms. He was laughing. And I think it was at me.

I swam away a little bit and dunked under to rinse off the sand and came up face-first, smoothing back my hair. Then I stood there and tried to act natural as Matt waded through the white water toward me.

"Leave it to Lexi to be the first one in!" he said, laughing and shaking his head.

"Early bird gets the worm!" I said. *Lame. So lame!*

Matt dove under and popped up about ten feet from me, floating on his back with his feet in the air. I wasn't sure if I should swim to him or stay put.

29

The sun beat down on me hard, and I wondered if I'd be okay for just a few minutes without sunscreen. I mean, I couldn't get that burned while I was underwater, right? I ducked under and swam out toward Matt, surfacing near him but not too close.

"Freezing!" he called.

"Is it?" I hadn't really noticed. I guess I was just numb. Or maybe I had more important things on my mind, like how cute Matt looked with his hair wet! But I suddenly realized I was freezing.

"Yeah. I don't think I can even stay in. My feet are numb. Wanna get out?"

I looked to shore. Emma and the others were standing, chatting with the boys. No one else had come in.

I shrugged. "It feels kind of good. And this way, by the time July rolls around, it's gonna feel like the Caribbean to us."

Matt laughed and shook his head. "Always planning ahead."

"It's my trademark!" I said, and I dove under again. I had to keep moving or I would freeze to death, that was for sure.

I came up, and Matt said, "Want to try and ride a wave in?"

"Okay."

It took a few attempts, but we both finally timed it right and got a good ride back to shore. We landed in a heap, laughing, at everyone's feet. Katie squealed and jumped away from us.

"How can you guys even put your feet in there? It's so cold! Even the drops from the spray feel freezing on my legs!"

Matt and I both shrugged and laughed. "I have to go back in and rinse off," I said. I stumbled back into the water and dove under a wave, then I paddled a bit, shook the sand out of my suit and my hair, and then made my way back in, careful not to get covered in sand again.

Out of the water, I dashed to my towel, partly because I was freezing and partly because I didn't need those guys seeing me in my too-small, unstylish, soaking-wet bathing suit from last summer! Snug and warming up, I walked slowly back to the group, where Matt was standing with his arms folded across his chest, shivering. His lips were actually bluish!

"Oh, Matt! You're freezing! Don't you have a towel?" I asked.

He laughed, but he shivered as he tried to talk. "It's at the other end of the beach. We wanted to be

31

away from people, so we could throw the football around, but it's pretty far."

The poor guy. "Here," I said impulsively. "You can use mine." I unwrapped myself and handed it toward him.

"No, you need it. That's okay. I'm fine. I'll warm right up in the sun."

"I insist!" I said. "Even for a minute. And you can take off the T-shirt, so you don't have that wet, cold fabric next to your skin."

"Nah, I'm okay. Here, I'll just use it to blot my face and hair a little. Thanks," he said. It warmed my heart to see my towel being used by Matt Taylor, love of my life. I was happy to have been able to help and happy that he accepted. It's like my mom always reminds us: You should accept people's help when they offer because it makes them feel good too.

I crossed my arms and waited to get my towel back. The sun felt good, and now I remembered again that I needed sunscreen. Darn it! But I didn't want to leave while Matt was still standing there.

"Thanks," he said again, handing my towel back. He looked a tiny bit warmer but not much. I was grateful to have the towel to hide behind again and especially to be able to cover up my shoulders, which were feeling warm and pinchy in the sun. "What are you guys doing about lunch? We're going to go to the snack bar," he said.

"Um." I looked at the others. "We could do that, I think. . . . Hey, guys? Want to go to the snack bar with the boys for lunch? When are you going?" I asked Matt, turning back to him.

He was staring at my legs when I looked at him.

"Huh? Oh. When are we going?" he repeated, all weird and awkward.

Why had he been looking at my legs? I was dying to look down and see what was wrong. Did I have a huge bruise or something? Were they neon white like Dylan had said? Ugh.

"Maybe in, like, half an hour?" he suggested.

"Okay. Sounds good. See you up there," I agreed. I was dying to get rid of him so I could look at my legs.

Matt turned, and he and George and their friends began walking away from us and down the beach. Instantly, I looked at my legs to see what was wrong with them. But there was nothing. Nothing I could see. Except maybe that my legs are super-white?

"Mia? Is there anything funny about my legs?" I asked anxiously.

Mia sized me up, squinting. "No," she said after a minute. "A little pale, but otherwise . . . superlong and pretty gorgeous!"

I blushed. "Oh, please!" I said. But inside I wondered if maybe, just maybe, Matt had been checking me out? I hoped so!

Now was the time to get on some sunscreen. I ducked under the umbrella and began slathering myself. "Anyone else want some?" I called, waving the tube in the air.

"Sure, but I'll do your back first," offered Emma, reaching for the tube.

I shrieked then as the cold sunscreen hit my sizzling back.

"Oh, Lexi—Alexis! You waited too long. This is bad. You've already got a burn," she said, sliding my strap a little to the side.

"Well, thanks for putting on the stuff. By the way, your poor brother was so cold, he was shivering, but he won't take his wet T-shirt off," I told her.

Emma sighed. "I feel disloyal even saying it, but since you love him, I can tell you. He has a birthmark on his shoulder, and he's embarrassed by it. So he wears a T-shirt at the beach to hide it. Meanwhile, the shirt makes him hot in the sun and freezing when he gets it wet, so I just think he shouldn't bother."

"Oh," I said. Wow. Who knew boys were self-conscious too? "How big?" I asked. I couldn't help myself.

"I don't know. Like, the size of a hockey puck, maybe?"

Now a hockey puck might be a good reference for someone like Emma, who has three brothers, but for me that could mean the size of a quarter or the size of a pizza. "Is that big?" I asked.

Emma giggled. "Your turn," she said, handing me the tube of sunscreen and turning around. She lifted her hair so I could do her back. "A hockey puck is maybe a two-and-a-half-inch-wide circle."

"Huh." So not tiny but not overwhelming. It made me feel very protective toward Matt, thinking he was shy of something. Especially since he's so fit and has such a cute build. I couldn't help it. I blurted, "I had no idea boys cared about stuff like that!"

Emma laughed hard. "Alexis, you are too much! Boys are people too!"

"They are?" I asked and shook my head, only half joking. "I had no idea!"

CHAPTER 4

Marked

$\mathscr{L}$unch with the boys was fun, and I noted that Matt had changed into a new, dry T-shirt, despite the fact his friends were still shirtless. I felt a little twinge in my heart, thinking of his birthmark. I guess it made me feel better knowing it, since I'm pretty insecure these days about myself. I wished I could tell Matt that we were alike— tell him something I hate about myself (one of the many things)—but I couldn't think of how to do it without seeming like I was fishing for compliments or admitting Emma had told me something she shouldn't have.

I ate my French fries and hot dog in the sunshine and looked out at the beach below us, now much busier. The ocean was a sparkling navy blue, and the sky was baby blue, with just two white fluffy clouds, way off on the horizon. There was a light breeze, but the sun was still strong. I knew I'd need to reapply my sunscreen after lunch. I had just my T-shirt on, so my shoulders were okay for now, anyway, but I realized I should've brought a hat.

"Lexi?"

I turned and saw that Matt was offering me a French fry from the new order he'd just picked up.

"Oh, thanks!" I smiled and reached out toward the cardboard box.

But then . . . "Matt! She hates being called 'Lexi.' It's *'Alexis'*!" chided Emma.

I blushed instantly. "Oh, no! That's okay. . . ."

"She thinks it's babyish," said Katie in a disbelieving voice. "I totally disagree, though." She smiled at me and shook her head a little as she bit into her burger.

"Oh, I'm sorry!" blurted Matt. His face was bright red when I looked back at him.

"No! It's fine!" I protested.

"What?" Now Matt just looked confused.

I sighed. This was turning into a mess. "If someone has always called me 'Lexi,' it's fine. I just don't want new people calling me 'Lexi,'" I explained.

"That's not what you told us!" said Mia.

"Oh," said Matt. There was a pause. Then he said, "So what should I call you?"

"'Lexi' is fine," I said.

"Wait, it's fine for him but not us?" cried Emma indignantly. "You said we couldn't call you that anymore, and it's been really hard!" This was the kind of thing that made her mad about me liking Matt—my double standards. Oops.

I sighed; I just wanted this conversation over with. "No, it's fine for everyone. Whatever. Never mind about the whole thing," I said, embarrassed now.

Matt's blush had faded, but he said, "I'll call you 'Alexis.'"

"Thanks," I said. But deep inside I kind of like that he calls me "Lexi." Too late for that now, I guess.

"Anyone up for some football?" George yelled from down in the sand.

We all agreed to try and cleaned up our lunch and headed off to their end of the beach, where there was some space. It crossed my mind that it was time to reapply a little sunscreen, but I didn't want to seem like a sunscreen nerd, so I just kind of looked at my bag and followed along with everyone else.

Now I am not a football person. My dad isn't into it, and I don't have any brothers. I don't understand how it is played or how you can even tell who is winning. But let me say this: It is my new favorite sport. Know why? Cute guys put their arm around you in the huddle!

I was on Matt's team, of course, and when we would huddle to discuss our strategy, he'd pull me in next to him and hang his arm across my shoulders. Granted, his other arm was across George's shoulders, but still! It felt really cozy and I loved it. We played for about an hour, and toward the end, I was kind of getting the hang of it: the running, the crossing lines, the tagging.

"Lexi—I mean, Alexis—you're pretty good at this!" Matt huffed after one of our last plays. "Must be those long legs of yours!" he said impulsively, and then he blushed and turned away.

I was dumbstruck. So he had been checking out my legs! And maybe not because they were neon white. I couldn't hold back my grin.

On the next play, we broke from our huddle and started out. We were tied, and this could be the end. I was going to go long for a pass from Matt, who was our quarterback, of course. But before he got a chance to throw, two of his friends on the other team executed a move they'd obviously planned, where they ran in and pulled Matt's T-shirt up from behind and over his head so he couldn't see. He still had the ball, and he kind of lamely tossed it, and guess what? I caught it! I couldn't believe it! Everyone was so busy laughing at Matt with his shirt over his head that I saw an opportunity and took off running! Quickly, the other team realized what was happening, but I was too far gone. I ran as fast as possible over the bumpy sand, and even though my bathing suit was riding way up, I didn't stop until I crossed the end line.

"Touchdown!" I yelled, spiking the ball proudly into the sand.

Most of my team came racing down the beach, whooping and hollering, and they grabbed me, and we danced around. But where was Matt?

I came up for air and looked for him. He was still back at the other end of the beach, his T-shirt in his hand, yelling at one of the guys who pulled it over his head.

"What's going on there?" I asked Katie.

"Oh, he's mad at that guy for yanking off his shirt. I think it ripped or something." She shrugged.

But inside, I wondered if it was because he was embarrassed. I felt bad for him, so I looked away.

"Let's hit the water!" cried Mia.

I was all hot and sandy from my sprint, so I was up for it. I took one look backward at Matt, and when I didn't catch his eye, I jogged down the beach with the others, to put our shirts and cover-ups down and to head into the water.

The water felt colder than before when I plunged in this time, but it was also a relief. The other girls shrieked and wound up not coming in; they just splashed some water on their faces and washed the sand off their legs. I lazed around for a minute, getting all the sand off me. I had to rub my skin kind of gingerly because it was feeling a little sensitive. Then I got out. It wasn't any fun without Matt, and I was too cold to stay in alone.

I blotted myself off and put on some more sunscreen, then I sat on my towel under our umbrella to do some Sudoku. I find numbers so relaxing that an hour could easily pass for me, doing these little puzzles. The other girls were chatting and reading, and after a bit, George wandered down the beach and sat on Katie's towel for a chat. I looked up, but when I didn't see Matt with him, I just hunkered back into my book.

But a few words caught my attention at one point, so I perked up to hear what George was saying.

". . . so mad. He was mortified about his shirt coming off. . . ."

Ugh! I knew what he was talking about now. Poor Matt! I wished there was a way to let him know that I, at least, hadn't seen his birthmark and that even if I had, I wouldn't care.

"He's just got to get over that!" piped Emma.

I sensed an opportunity to send Matt a message via George, so I inched over and said, "Who get over what?"

George looked at Emma, as if wondering if he should tell me, and Emma said, "Matt and his birthmark."

"Oh." I waved my hand breezily. "Everyone's got *something*, right? I mean, who cares? Seriously. So not a big deal. Especially . . ." I paused. I wasn't sure I really wanted to let George know how I felt about Matt.

But Katie jumped in and teased, "Especially when someone's as handsome as Matt, right, Alexis?"

I just grinned and shrugged.

George smiled.

Message sent, I thought happily.

"Gosh, Alexis, you're pretty fried," George said suddenly, squinting at me under the umbrella. He

42

wasn't teasing. He actually looked concerned.

My hand flew to my face. "Really? That noticeable?"

The girls looked closely at me. "Yeah." Emma nodded. "That might hurt later."

I looked at my watch. Three thirty. "What time are we thinking of staying until?" I craned my head to look down the beach, to see if I might see Matt. Maybe I could wander down there one more time.

Katie stood up and stretched. "My mom had said we should leave by four since she has a date with Jeff tonight and she needs to get back."

Katie's mom is dating one of our teachers at school, Mr. Green, and it's still funny to hear her refer to him by his first name. "Hey," she added. "I forgot the reason we came in the first place. Any cupcake ideas?"

We all looked around the beach for a minute, and then Mia said, "Umbrellas? We could use those little tropical drink thingies."

Emma said, "Beach towels? We could use Airheads candies—they're little and rectangular, and they kind of look like beach towels!"

Katie laughed and clapped her hands. "Great!"

"Now we can write off our lunch as a business expense!" I said happily.

Everyone laughed, and we all began to pack up. I pulled on my skirt, shook out my towel, and put my book and pencil back in my bag. We were chatting about homework and exams, and Mia said, "Ugh. I am dreading that vocabulary test on Monday."

"Oh, well, it's on Tuesday, so don't worry," I comforted her.

But Emma said, "No, it's on Monday."

I shook my head. "It's the twenty-eighth. That's Tuesday."

"That's Monday," Emma said quietly.

George and Katie had been chatting, but now they turned to us, and Katie asked, "Are you talking about what day it is?"

I nodded. I was starting to get a queasy feeling in my stomach all of a sudden. "When is the twenty-eighth?" I asked weakly.

"Monday!" they said in unison, and they laughed and turned back to chatting.

I sat down heavily on the sand. "Wait. Wait. Are you sure?"

Emma looked down at me and nodded sadly, like she hated to break the news.

"But I didn't even bring my book home!" I wailed. Vocab is not one of my best subjects, either.

I put my forehead in my hand. Oh boy.

Emma squatted down, "Lexi, it's okay. You can come over and study with me tomorrow, okay? Don't worry."

"Thanks, Em," I said, not even caring what she called me. "I can't believe I spaced out like that! It's so not like me!"

"I know," she agreed. "Maybe your mind is just on other things right now," she added.

"It shouldn't be!" I said gruffly. I was mad at myself.

"I'm going to go tell my mom we're ready," said Katie, and she and George headed off across the sand.

Sighing, I stood up and dusted the sand off my legs. I had a lot of work to do, to get stuff finished tonight so I could study at Emma's tomorrow.

"Don't worry, Alexis, you'll do great," comforted Mia.

I groaned. "I doubt it," I said.

"Hey," Emma said.

"Hey," said a voice behind me. Matt!

I whirled around, an idiotic grin on my face. "Hi!" I said. "I thought you left!"

He had his T-shirt back on. "Nah. Probably going to take one more swim. All those guys are such wimps, they won't go in with me. I thought you might." He smiled his lopsided grin at me. "But I can see you're all dressed and ready to go, so we can do it another time."

"Oh. Well . . . actually . . ." I looked down at my packed bag.

"Are you going to a party?" he asked.

Confused, I shook my head. "No. Why?"

"Oh . . . just . . . you look nice. That's all." He shrugged.

Darn this skirt! It was wrong, wrong, wrong. All I wanted to do when I got home was clean out my closet, and now I had to do homework, all because of this stupid vocab exam!

"Oh. Thanks," I said, shrugging, trying to play it cool when inside I was totally stressed out.

"Ready, girls?" Mrs. Brown asked, arriving at our little group. She said hi to Matt and asked if she could help with our gear, and then she headed up to bring the car around.

"Do you have a ride?" Emma asked him.

"Yeah, I'm good. Thanks. See you guys."

I wished there was something I could say to Matt that conveyed everything I felt right then, like, *You're so cute and nice and fun, I don't care about your stupid birthmark, I wish I could swim with you now for an hour, and I hate this skirt, but I'm too tall to wear anything else.*

Instead, I said, "Bye! See you tomorrow, maybe!"

And he said, "Bye, Alexis!"

No more "Lexi," I guess.

I've never hated my name so much as I did right then.

CHAPTER 5

Burned

Despite the cool shower, some lotion, a ton of aloe, and a light cotton nightgown, there was nothing I could do that night but toss and turn in my bed, uncomfortable from my sunburn and my aching legs.

I had fried myself, it turned out. And worse, I had applied what little sunscreen I *did* use in such a sloppy fashion that I had big, dorky, white (non-burned) streaks across my chest and forehead and parts of my arms. I looked like a total freak.

"Holy raspberry-vanilla swirl!" Dylan had laughed when I got out of the shower that night.

I glared at her and stalked back to my room to google sunburn remedies.

Finding little of use, I asked my mom for an

aspirin (it's supposed to help both the burn and the achy legs, but it didn't), listened to my mom's lecture about skin cancer and sun damage and how surprised she was at my "uncharacteristic disorganization," did a bunch of homework, and went to bed. (Notice I didn't say "went to sleep," because I didn't!)

The next morning, I was grumpy when I got up and made grumpier still when I checked my texts.

Katie had sent a Cupcake Club request for me to finalize the proposal for the beach barbecue cupcakes for her neighbor ASAP, because they might go with the bakery in town. Mia had forwarded a flyer for a bake sale fund-raiser at the shelter where the vet for her dogs, Tiki and Milkshake, worked, to see if we'd be willing to donate cupcakes. And Emma had texted to say she couldn't meet this afternoon so how early could I come this morning?

"Ugh!" I yelled.

I replied yes to Emma immediately, because what else could I say? She was doing me a favor, after all. I wanted to ask her if Matt would be there, so I'd know how much time I should spend trying to find something decent to wear, but I knew she'd be annoyed if I asked. We'd seen a little too much of him yesterday for her liking, and I didn't want to push it.

I started rifling through my drawers, looking for things I'd avoided in the past because they were too big. Also, I needed something that wasn't tight on my shoulders or chest, where my burn was the worst. I got so frustrated at one point that I dumped my drawers out onto my made bed and scrambled everything up willy-nilly. I guess I must've been making a lot of noise because Dylan came in to gloat in my doorway. She leaned against the doorframe, smiling a little.

"Need my help again?" She smirked.

I growled at her. "No, thank you!"

"Looks like ya do!" she singsonged. "Don't deny it! You know I can help you!"

I whirled around. "Oh yeah? You can help me? Okay. Try this one on. I need an outfit that won't hurt my streaky sunburn, that will, in fact, *hide* my streaky sunburn; that doesn't look too dressy or too casual; that isn't too small for me; that says, 'Hi, I'm here to study with Emma!' but can also say, 'Hi, Matt! I think you're cute and I hope you like me, too!' Oh yeah, and this needs to be something that you, Mom, or I already own so I can put it on in the next five minutes!" I stood with my hands on my hips, huffing and puffing, glaring wildly at Dylan.

"Whoa!" she said, holding her palms up toward me. "I do love a challenge," she said after a pause. "I have just the thing!" She turned and left the room.

"Just the thing, just the thing. Ha!" I muttered. "Unless it's Harry Potter's invisibility cloak!" I tapped my foot angrily and decided I'd give her exactly one minute before I pulled on sweats and called it a day.

Thirty-seven seconds later, Dylan came back with a triumphant look on her face. She was holding something behind her back and said, "They really should do a reality show about me. Like, *Wardrobe Smackdown* or something. Close your eyes and put out your hands."

Annoyed, I played along and closed them.

I felt her lay something in my arms, and she said, "Okay."

I opened my eyes and there was *the most* adorable, supersoft, thick, brushed-cotton, blue-and-white-striped T-shirt dress. Did I mention how soft it was?

"Is this a nightgown?" I asked, holding it up and shaking it out to its full length.

Dylan shook her head. "It's from one of those French sailor shirt companies. They're making dresses now. Remember when I got it for my birthday from Grandma? I've been saving it."

"Oh," I said, moving to hand it back to her. But she pushed it back toward me.

"No," she said. "You really need it today. Just be careful with it, okay?"

I hesitated. Did I really want the responsibility of wearing Dylan's new dress? I looked at her, and she was smiling at me. I thought again of my mom's advice to let people do nice things for you, and I smiled back.

"This is really awesome, Dylan. Thank you. Thanks so much!" I impulsively hugged her, and she hugged me back. "Easy! I'm still sunburned," I said with a laugh. Dylan pulled away and I stared at her. "Why are you being so nice?" I had to ask.

Dylan sighed. "Because I remember what it feels like when your body betrays you. It stinks." She laughed a little. "I wished I had a big sister who could've helped me, back then."

"Huh," I said. "Sorry. And thanks."

"No problemo," said Dylan, and she left the room, calling over her shoulder, "Wear it with your blue Tom's!"

I slid the dress on over my head, and it looked awesome and felt even better. My mood improved immediately by about 100 percent. I jammed my comfy Tom's onto my feet, grabbed my backpack, and headed out without answering Mia's or Katie's texts.

At Emma's, we drilled each other on vocabulary for a whole hour. She did well and I did not. We took a break to eat some chocolate-chip pancakes Mrs. Taylor had made, and I brought up the bake sale.

"Oh yeah, I saw that. What do you think?" asked Emma.

I cut a bite of pancake and chewed thoughtfully. "I suppose it would be good PR for us. . . ."

"Wait, that means 'public relations,' right?"

I nodded and swallowed. "Yes. Good to get our name out there, good to have the Cupcake Club be seen as charitable. I mean, the only bummer is we can't take a tax write-off for the donation because we don't pay taxes!"

Emma laughed. "Wait, *what*? You are way ahead of me, sister!"

I shook my head and smiled. "Never mind. Just thinking out loud. Business talk." Then I dropped my voice to a whisper to make a confession. "You know, I like the *idea* of being charitable as much as anyone, and I think it's superimportant. It's just sometimes it's kind of a hassle, you know? Like the timing of this thing, right after tests, right when we have to bake for the barbecue too? Not the greatest."

Emma shook her head at me and wagged her finger scoldingly. "You are bad, missy! Think of all those little critters who need our help!" Emma loves animals; she even has a dog-walking business on the side.

"I know," I agreed with a sigh. "Don't tell anyone what I said, okay?"

"I promise," said Emma. "So we'll say yes?"

I nodded. "Yes. And let's make them cute while we're at it. Maybe little doggy and kitty faces on top?"

"Totally! That *would* be cute!"

"We just need to figure out which night to bake them. I'll text the others when I get home. And I have to do that proposal for the barbecue, too."

"*And* you need to do your schoolwork, which is really more important! But I don't need to tell you that. You're the most organized of us all!"

"Hmph," I said. "I'm not so sure these days. I'm feeling a little distracted."

"Maybe you're just overtired . . . ," teased Emma. My mom's big explanation for all of our grouchiness or bad behavior growing up was that we were overtired.

I giggled at the reference. "Yeah. Or maybe I forgot to take my vitamins!" That was her other one. I sighed and stood up to clear our plates.

"Thanks," said Emma. "Ready for round two? I have a half an hour more till I have to leave for my aunt's house. I'll quiz you."

"Okay . . ." I sighed again as I put the dishes into the Taylors' dishwasher. It was unlike me to be so unmotivated to study, even if it was vocabulary.

"Are you okay, Lexi?" asked Emma, looking at me in concern.

I nodded. "I'm just really tired, is all." And it was true.

She nodded sympathetically. "Probably all that growing."

"Yeah, plus all the work ahead of me: the vocabulary exam, my history paper, the barbecue proposal, baking the samples for that, baking for the animal shelter. Then on top of that, I really need to clean out my closet and find a few new things to wear, which sounds unimportant but is probably the most important of all! Not having even the simplest thing to wear that fits is really frustrating!"

"Can I help?" asked Emma.

I shook my head. "Not right now. I'll let you know."

"Don't forget, we can do some baking without you, since you're always doing the extra work on the office side and the purchasing."

"Thanks," I agreed. "I might actually take you up on that this week."

Emma picked up her vocabulary book and wiggled it at me. "Ready?"

"Ready as I'll ever be!" I chirped, all fake-energetic.

"Oh boy, I hope not!" Emma laughed.

CHAPTER 6

Teen Angst

That afternoon, instead of working on my history paper, I worked on the Cupcake Club's proposal for Mrs. Dreher's barbecue cupcakes. I had to call Katie to get some estimates on quantities of the "sand" sugar, and that took a little while because we chatted about other stuff. Then I had to go on another website to get some pricing for cocktail umbrellas, and then I found these cute cupcake wrappers, and pretty soon I was looking at teen clothes websites, and the next thing I knew, I had wasted an hour and a half. Yes, *me*! Alexis Becker! Wasting time. Imagine that.

When I realized how much time had passed while I was online, I quickly got organized and whipped up the proposal. Luckily, I sent it to the others for proofreading because Mia quickly caught the fact that I hadn't priced out the frosting!

What was the world coming to?

Alexis Becker wasting time? Making business mistakes? What next? Getting Fs in school? I sure hope not.

I edited the proposal and e-mailed it to Mrs. Dreher, then I got to work on my history paper. When my mom called me down for dinner at exactly 6:30 p.m. (as always), I was happy for the break. But when I discovered we were having kale with our fish, I was not as happy.

"Mother. I cannot eat this stuff. It smells like a dead animal," I said dramatically.

"Alexis!" my father said sharply. "Do not be rude to your mother. She has worked hard to put this food on the table, and I won't have you being disrespectful."

I sighed. He was right. "I'm sorry, Mom, but seriously. Do I have to eat it?"

"I love it!" said Dylan, wolfing it down. She's majorly into veggies and healthy food, too, these days. It's all part of her acting grown-up thing. I rolled my eyes.

My mom turned to me and said, "I guess you don't have to eat all of it, but you must take a bite.

Research shows that it can take up to seven times of trying a new food before children start to like it. Anyway, I always thought you were my good little veggie eater, Lexi!"

I made a face and decided to get the bite over with. But first I announced, "I am not going by 'Lexi,' anymore, Mother."

My parents exchanged a look that annoyed me.

"Why?" asked my father with a small smile.

"It's babyish," I declared.

"Ah," said my father, nodding. He looked like he was going to smile again, but he didn't. I looked at my mom, and she had the same kind of expression on her face, which bugged me.

I pinched my nose with my fingers and gulped down a smallish bite of kale. But uh-oh! The taste came through, even with my nose pinched shut, and I couldn't help it, but I gagged.

"Alexis! For heaven's sake!" cried my mother as I spit the kale into my napkin.

"Sorry!" I croaked as I hurriedly took a sip of my milk to get ride of the taste.

"Alexis, what's gotten into you this week?" my father asked seriously. "I hear you're forgetting books at school, falling behind in your work, forgetting your sunscreen . . . now you're being rude at the dinner table and asking us to change what we call you. Oh!" He smacked his hand on his forehead and shook his head, rolling his eyes to the ceiling. "What am I thinking? It's teen angst. Of course!"

"Oh no! Not again!" cried my mom, glancing at Dylan.

Dylan looked huffy. "Don't drag me into this!" she said indignantly.

"I'm not even a teenager yet!" I protested.

"Here we go," Dylan said, rolling her eyes.

"Chronological age has nothing to do with the onset of teen angst," said my mother knowledgably. "That's what they say at parenting class."

"Well, I have no angst," I said. "I just hate kale."

My mom and dad looked at each other and then burst our laughing.

"You two are so annoying," I said, and I finished my halibut and asked to be excused to clear my plate. As I left the room, I heard my mom remark, "One finally coming out of teen angst and now one heading into it."

"We can't catch a break," replied my dad.

"Hey! I'm not the problem!" Dylan said.

I rolled my eyes and went back upstairs to try to finish my homework and studying.

❁

Now, I am all about efficiency and order and neatness. A place for everything and everything in its place. A stitch in time saves nine. Failing to plan is planning to fail. Those are some of my mottoes.

But maybe they shouldn't be anymore.

Like, first, I forget my vocabulary book, then I forget my sunscreen, and now there's the growing pile of clothes that don't fit me. It was on my bed, but by the time I had finished my work and was ready to crawl in to go to sleep, I really didn't feel like dealing with the pile. So I kind of scooped it up and dumped it in the corner of my room. The next morning, when I was getting dressed for school, I discovered that another pair of my shorts didn't fit, so I chucked them on top of the pile. Things were definitely not in their place, and no stitches were being saved. Where was the old me, and who was this new person I was becoming?

Another one of my mottoes is: Quack! I know it sounds dumb, but it's something my mom always tells us. When something is bothering you, sometimes you just need to let it roll off your back, like water rolls off a duck's back. Now we just say "Quack!" as shorthand for that expression.

But at school that morning, I was on my way to my class from my locker when I passed Olivia Allen, the head of the BFC (Best Friends Club, which I am decidedly not in. It's sort of the cool girls–mean girls club, and Olivia sets the tone).

Olivia looked at me and burst out laughing. "Alexis! OMG! Haven't you ever heard of sunscreen?" She looked around to see if any of her buddies were there to share in her laughter, but they weren't.

"What*ever*," I muttered, and kept on walking, but inside, I was enraged. I thought my burn had faded enough by now, but maybe it was just that I had gotten used to it. Also, I thought Olivia and I had made peace, so I wasn't sure why she was launching some new assault. I knew I should just say "Quack!," but she'd caught me off guard, and I was pretty vulnerable these days.

"Those are some serious freckles!" she continued.

Wait, *freckles*?

My second class was English, and I was really feeling skittery and nervous about the vocabulary test, but I did a quick detour to the girls' bathroom to look in the mirror.

I stared at my skin, tilting my head every which way. I've always had freckles, as far as I know, but maybe they were a little more . . . pronounced all of a sudden? Were they darker? Were there more of them? And if so, was there anything I could do about it? Oh, who knows!

I hurried out and ran the last few paces to my English classroom, just as Mrs. Carr was beginning to close the door.

Now, I am a numbers person, and though my parents tell me all the time that being good at numbers doesn't mean you're not good at words, I kind of disagree, just based on how my friends and I all do at school. I mean, of course I usually get honors grades in the writing classes, like history and English, but more like B pluses than As. But today, I realized with a sinking feeling that I might not even be getting a B plus.

As I progressed through the test, I felt like I hadn't even seen some of these words before! See, usually, I would have made flashcards from the book and tested myself that way. And maybe it's the act of writing the words down that helps cement them in my mind or something, but without the book at home this weekend, I couldn't do that. As my already-shaky confidence slipped, I started to really tank. I actually thought I might cry at one point when I looked around the room, stumped for the third time, and saw everyone scribbling away on their papers, as if they couldn't get their right answers down fast enough. This was just not me! Alexis Becker doesn't do badly in school!

I finished up the best I could, guessing when possible and giving partial answers. At the end of the allotted time, I was just glad to be finished with it. I gave Mrs. Carr a mournful look as she collected my test, but she didn't notice. I sighed heavily.

After class, I went to Mrs. Carr's desk to explain that I had forgotten my book. Luckily, I am usually a diligent student so teachers don't really look at me as a slacker.

"Um, Mrs. Carr?" I said.

"Yes, Alexis?" She smiled at me pleasantly.

"Uh . . . I think I kind of tanked the test," I said, feeling a deep blush rise to the roots of my hair. Maybe she wouldn't notice because of my darn sunburn.

Mrs. Carr chuckled. "I'm sure you did just fine," she said. The flip side of being a good student is that you get a bit of a reputation as a perfectionist. This would *not* be working in my favor right now.

"Well, I forgot to bring the book home this weekend, and though I did study, I wasn't able to do my usual study system." That sounded good. I looked at her hopefully.

She shuffled the papers into a pile and tapped them on her desk to even them out. Then she looked me right in the eye. "Alexis, why don't I give your test a look tonight, and we can see what happened. I'm sure it wasn't as bad as you think."

"I'm sure it was, but okay."

"If it's a fail, we'll cross that bridge when we come to it," she said kindly.

A *fail*? OMG. I have never failed anything in my life! I gulped and then smiled nervously. "Thanks." I walked blindly to my next class, my knees feeling like jelly.

At lunch, I was superdistracted.

"Cute shirt!" said Mia.

"Thanks. It's my mom's," I said absently.

"Still having problems with the clothing?" she asked.

I nodded.

"Why don't I come over and help you clean out your clothes?" she suggested excitedly. "Then we can figure out a few things you should get to fill in."

I looked at her. This was the opportunity of a lifetime. To have Mia's eye laser-focused on my wardrobe? People would pay top dollar for that one day. Normally, I would jump at the chance, but I

65

was feeling so swamped. "Thanks! That would be great. I wish we could do it soon, but it's kind of a crazy week."

"I know. Thanks for saying yes on the animal shelter bake sale, by the way. We don't have to make a lot. We'll just have a massive baking session on Friday. We'll do the Mona minis, the shelter, and maybe bake the cupcakes for Sunday, but we can decorate them on Saturday? Then, while stuff is baking, I can help you with your clothes, okay? We'll get organized!" She grinned at me, knowing that getting organized is usually my favorite thing on Earth.

But right now it kind of sounded like a hassle.

Katie joined us and did kind of a double take when she saw me. "Oh, Lexi! When did you get so many freckles?" she asked.

"Ugh. Thanks for reminding me!" I said. "Olivia was the first to point them out this morning. Great way to start the day."

"Sorry!" said Katie. She glanced uneasily at Mia. "It's just . . . I never really noticed them before. Maybe now that the burn is fading . . ."

"It's not that bad. Don't worry, Lexi—" Mia said.

Katie smacked her forehead. "Gosh, should I just start over? Can I go back and put my lunch away and come in again?" She laughed, and we all laughed then, and the tension was put to rest. Katie's too nice for me to get mad at her for real.

"Don't worry about it," I said generously. "Things may be tough, but I still have my sense of humor! *And my freckles!*" I joked. We all knew that despite my cranky little challenges, this was not a tough life.

Emma joined us, and we went through the weekend plans and then discussed our week's worth of exams. With my history paper ready to turn in, and the vocabulary test behind me, what was left was just the stuff I was prepared for, so I did feel a bit better.

Katie informed us that Mrs. Dreher had called last night to say the cupcake proposal looked great, and she was going to e-mail me today to tell us to go ahead. We whooped and high-fived. It was a big job and would be good money and good neighborhood exposure for us. She also said that Mrs. Dreher had invited us all to the party, since Katie and Mrs. Brown were already going.

"And guess what?" continued Katie. "I have more great news!"

"What?"

"George told me he's invited, since Ben Dreher

is in his class, and all his friends are invited too, so that means Matt's going!"

"Yay!" I squealed. "Sorry, Emma!" I said.

But Emma waved her hand. "It's fine. He and I are getting along pretty well these days, anyway. Maybe it's because I'm all mature and cool now," she joked.

"Maybe it's because he likes your friends," teased Mia, raising her eyebrows at me.

I blushed again, looked down at my tray. "I just hope he likes freckles," I said.

CHAPTER 7

F

So I failed the test.

Yes, there's a first time for everything, it's true, and there are exceptions to every rule, et cetera, et cetera. But the bottom line is Beckers don't fail. Our family motto is: The Beckers try harder. I mean, that's a winning motto if ever I heard one. I have never brought home an F, or even a D, on anything. I think I've gotten two Cs in my life. One was on a pop quiz and the other was on a history test I'd had after I'd been out with strep throat for two days.

Mrs. Carr was very kind about it when she called me up to her desk before class on Tuesday. "Alexis, you are usually an excellent student. I know this is not your normal work. I will make an exception this time and allow you to retake the test on Thursday, and I will award you half credit for every point. That will bring you out of the F zone and more into a C. It's the best I can offer you. I will have to offer it to all the students in the class to improve their grade, just to be fair."

I nodded miserably. It was all I could do not to cry. Mrs. Carr being nice about it almost made it worse. It was pretty huge that she was allowing me to retake the same test, but a C? But what could I do? "Thank you so much, Mrs. Carr. I will study so hard tonight and tomorrow, and I will do much better on the retest. I promise. Thank you."

In a daze, clutching the test, I slunk to my desk and dropped into my seat. I jammed the paper into my binder and spent the rest of the class trying to think about how I was going to tell my parents.

That afternoon, I certainly did not forget to bring home my vocabulary book. In fact, I spent an extra half an hour cleaning out my locker before I left school, so that everything was in its place. At home, I diligently wrote out note cards for all the vocabulary words, and then I randomly interspersed them with my science note cards and quizzed myself for two hours. Academically, I felt more in control than I had in a week.

But meanwhile, the pile of clothes in my room had grown to new heights. In my mind I was starting to call it the Hulk. It was taking on a life of its own. I was down to two outfits that I was rotating, washing one each night. My mom's turquoise T-shirt was officially mine now (I couldn't even get excited about it, really, since now I was almost sick of it).

And I had to tell my parents about the F.

My mom made a Spanish egg-and-potato *frittata* for dinner, with a microgreens salad. I ate it all and remarked a couple of times on how delicious it was. I didn't want to overdo it, because I didn't want her to think I was buttering her up, even though I kind of was. The *frittata* was pretty good, actually, so I wasn't making it up. The microgreens, not so much, but at least I didn't have to choke down any kale.

Dylan cleared her plate first and went up to finish her studying. That left me and my parents alone at the table, thank goodness. They were chatting excitedly about a ballet they were going to see in the city next week. It had gotten a good review in the paper today, and my parents were psyched they had "the hot tickets" in hand already. I hated to burst their bubble, but it was the perfect time to strike: happy news, full bellies. Ideal.

"Um . . . guys?" I began.

They looked at me with identically pleasant expressions on their faces, right at the same time, and suddenly, I was so ashamed. I started to cry. It wasn't for sympathy; it was because I felt guilty. Here I was, living this great life they'd built for me, and I was about to tell them I'd just failed a test. I mean, how easy is it to do well on a test? But I'd been disorganized and selfish and a slacker.

"Alexis! What ever is the matter?" asked my mom.

My dad reached out to pat my arm. "What is it, Lexi?"

I didn't bother to correct him on the name. Not only would it have been a tactical error, but I was actually comforted to hear that name right now. It made me feel less guilty, like I was still a little kid or something.

"I failed a test!" I sobbed.

There was a shocked silence.

"What?" My mom blinked.

Oh no. Are they going to freak out? I wondered. *Will I be grounded for life?*

"What subject?" asked my dad, all businesslike.

"It was . . . a vocabulary test. In my English class."

I sniffled. "I thought the test was Tuesday, so I didn't bring my book home over the weekend. I didn't do my usual note cards. I just . . . I tanked," I cried. "I'm so sorry. It's so embarrassing!"

My parents looked at each other, and I looked back and forth between them. I suddenly realized that they had no idea what to do or say. They were just as baffled by the news as I was; I'd just had longer to get used to the idea. No one in our family ever failed anything!

My dad cleared his throat. "Well, what did the teacher say?" They looked at me expectantly. Thank goodness I'd gone to the teacher!

"She said I can retake it on Thursday. The same test. It's because I'm usually a good student."

They smiled in relief. "Well done, honey," said my dad.

"Yes, good for you for handling it!" said my mom.

"The only thing is . . . ," I continued, wincing now. "I can only get half credit back on the retake. So"—I started to sob again—"the best I can do is a C!"

There was a pause while the only noise in the room were my sniffles. It was mortifying. I was waiting for yelling and reprimands, but none were coming.

Finally, my dad said, "Alexis, you are an excellent student. You've never given us a moment's trouble in school. Is everything okay?"

"Yes, everything's fine. I've just . . . I'm . . . I just feel superdistracted and disorganized these days. I mean, this sounds really dumb, but none of my clothes fit, and my knees are hurting all the time, and now I have this dumb sunburn, and we have all this baking to do, and my exams . . . And I'm just so tired all the time!" I might as well lay it all out on the table, I figured.

"Honey, I'm sorry," said my mom. "How can we help?"

I looked up. "Wait, I'm not punished?" I asked.

"Punished?" My dad laughed. "Why would we punish you?"

"For the F!" I said.

"Alexis, you're punishing yourself more than we ever would," said my mom. "They're your grades. I mean, certainly, if you were a poor student, or if it was a pattern, or you seemed to not care or to be blowing things off . . . then we'd be talking punishment. But you're a good kid, and you do try hard. Harder!" she joked, referring to our motto. "What can we do to help you?"

I sighed, feeling emotionally spent. "I just need

to get through this week of exams, then I have my baking on Friday. Mia's going to help me clean out my clothes. I might need some money to get a few new things at Big Blue. I mean, I have a little money from Grandma and from the Cupcake Club, but . . ."

"We can give you some money for new clothes," said my dad. "It's not like it's a splurge. It sounds like you need them."

My mom nodded and patted my hand. Then she said, "It sounds like you were troubled about the test, so you reached out to your teacher and she helped you. And then you were upset and you told us, and we can help you, at least with the other stuff. Remember, Alexis, that's the best thing you can do when things are troubling you in life: ask for help. Especially ask a grown-up, okay?" She looked at me.

Normally, I would have cringed at her little lecture, but right now I was just grateful. I nodded.

"As for your legs hurting, that might be due to your growth spurt, but let's take you in to see Dr. Stephens, just in case, okay?" Dad looked at my mom, who nodded again. "Maybe there's something you can be doing so it doesn't hurt as much."

"Now, would you like me to quiz you?" offered my mom.

I nodded and slowly stood up to clear.

"I'll do the dishes," said my dad.

Upstairs, my mom glanced around my room.

"Alexis, it *is* kind of a mess in here," she said. She perched on the edge of my bed while I sat in my swivel desk chair.

"I know," I said. "I just don't want to keep putting away the things that don't fit, and I don't know where else to put them."

"After I quiz you, I'll get some shopping bags, and we can pack them up and bring them downstairs, okay? This is a little depressing."

"What are we going to do with the clothes? Throw them away?"

My mom was shocked. "Absolutely not! We can give them away. Some of those things are brandnew!"

"Okay, sorry!" I said. "Who do you give them to?"

My mom bit her lip and thought for a second. "I used to drop them off at the shelter, but they closed that place. I'll ask around. I'm not really sure. I have some things I could pass along too. A few fashion choices that didn't work out, as Dylan was quick to point out," she said with a laugh.

I handed her the note cards and explained about the intermingled subjects.

She nodded and began the quizzing. After about forty-five minutes, we decided I was in pretty good shape. "There's the Alexis I know!" My mom beamed.

I smiled back, hoping she was right. Maybe I'd just had a crazy weekend. The ocean air tired me out, the sunburn, the distraction of the clothes not fitting. I was back on track, for sure.

We packed up the clothes, and while my mom brought them downstairs to the front hall, I took the opportunity to straighten up my desk. I love my desk, usually, but I've been too tired to clean it up lately, so it was piled with all the papers I'd used to review for exams, and all my pens and pencils were out of order, and stuff like that.

By the time my mom came back to say good night, I felt a lot better. It sounds dumb, but sometimes just getting things in order—cleaning up, organizing, feeling in control—can make everything seem a lot easier.

"Looks like things are back on track in here!" said my mom, bending down to plant a kiss on my forehead.

I smiled. "Yup."

"Good job, bunny," she said. She turned off the overhead light and stood in the doorway.

"Mom?" I asked.

"Yes, dear?"

"Is there a way to get rid of freckles?"

She laughed. "Not that I know of. But I think your freckles are cute!"

I made a gagging sound. "Barf. Please!"

"Oh, come on, Alexis. They're so natural-looking and pretty." She thought for a second. "I suppose if you wanted to tone them down, you could put a little tinted moisturizer over them or something, just for special occasions."

"Do you have any?"

"Yes, I'll leave it in your bathroom. You know, in some cultures, freckles are considered good luck. . . ."

"Where?" I demanded.

"Good night!" she trilled, and closed the door. I knew she was making it up, but I had to laugh.

I snuggled in and drifted off for a good, restful night's sleep.

Only that wasn't what I got.

At eleven thirty, my legs were aching so badly, they woke me up out of a dead sleep. I tried changing positions and rubbing them, and I even got up and stretched them out. None of that helped. It was a dull throbbing in my knees and in my shin bones that went on and on, occasionally turning into a piercing, stabbing feeling. Finally, I turned on the light. I was so tired and feeling really sorry for myself. I started calculating how many hours of sleep I'd get if I fell right back to sleep, and it was not much. I got up to google "aching legs," and that was when I heard a little tap on the door.

"Lexi?" It was my mom.

"Come in," I said.

"What are you doing?" She was in her night-gown and all squinty, which meant she'd taken out her contacts.

"My legs are killing me. It woke me up."

"Oh, sweetheart. I remember when that used to happen to me. My mom would rub them with lavender oil, and it did help a little. Want me to do that?" She yawned.

"No, that's okay, Mom. I can do it myself. Do you have any?"

She nodded and left the room, returning momentarily with a little brown bottle with a dropper in it. "It smells pretty strong so I brought you a towel to put down, too. Here, let me do it. Come on."

She laid the towel over my sheets and had me lie down, then she used the dropper to put some oil on each of my knees and began to massage them. It felt so, so good.

"Mom, thank youuuuuu," I whispered.

"Mmm hmm," she said. Her eyes were closed, and I could tell she was half-asleep herself. I felt guilty but not guilty enough to have her stop.

"You're the best mom ever," I said.

"I hope you remember that when your teen angst kicks in for real," she said, a half-smile on her face.

"Oh, please. I'm not going to have teen angst," I said.

"Right," Mom said.

CHAPTER 8

Worst Mom Ever

The rest of my exams went well, thank goodness, and I aced my vocab retest, though it was not much of a consolation, since my grade did average out to a C. I had to chalk it up to experience and move on, my dad said. My mom told me not to dwell on it, but not to let it happen again. Quack.

I was actually looking forward to Friday afternoon, even though the Cupcake Club had a lot of work to do. I needed Mia's help with my clothes cleanout ASAP, and I knew Saturday would give me an opportunity to shop with my friends and fill in the gaps in my wardrobe.

So that's why it hit me pretty hard when my mom announced on Thursday that we were going to visit my grandmother out in the country on Saturday.

"Bummer! I can't go!" I said. I love my grandma, and I hated to miss a trip to see her.

"It's not optional," said my mom. She continued folding the laundry.

Wait, is this a joke? "But, Mom! I'm going shopping with my friends on Saturday. Remember? I have the barbecue on Sunday, and I need something to wear."

"Grandma would love to take you shopping out there," said my mom with a chuckle. "And she pays!"

"Thanks, but no thanks," I said. "I have this all planned."

My mom stopped folding and looked at me. "It's not optional, I said. It's the only time we can get out there to celebrate Grandpa Jim's birthday, and I can hardly tell them you can't make it because you're going shopping!"

"You aren't serious? You're going to make me bag all my plans?"

"I'm sorry, but your friends will understand." My mom began folding again, which meant this conversation was over.

"This is totally unfair!" I yelled. "You're the worst mother in the whole world!" Then I stomped up the stairs and slammed my door.

Inside my room, I was fuming. How could she? She knew I had plans. Maybe not the specifics, but she had an idea! Why didn't she check with me first? Who did she think she was? I punched my pillow and went to kick the side of my bed, but decided against it. No point in hurting myself just because I was mad at her!

I flopped onto my bed and then crossed my arms, glaring at the ceiling. When I grow up, I will never, ever make plans for my kids without checking with them first! Ever!

There was a knock on the door.

"Go away!" I yelled.

"Jeez, it's me!" said Dylan.

"Fine. Whatever," I said.

The door opened, and she came in and then shut it behind her. "Mom's making you go to Grandma's?" she asked.

"What, you don't have to go?"

"Well, I told Mom I couldn't go because I had plans, but I actually just canceled them because I hadn't been out there in a while. Anyway, maybe Grandma will take me to the mall."

"Wait, first you didn't have to go because you had plans? And my plans don't count? And now you're bagging your friends so you can get free clothes out of Grandma?" I asked incredulously.

"Well, it's not exactly like that . . . ," said Dylan.

"Pretty much," I corrected her.

Dylan smiled. "I guess. I just wanted to say, I don't think you should have to go. I'll tell Mom that I'll go, and then the pressure will be off you."

I sat up. "Really? Why are you helping me?" I narrowed my eyes.

"Like I said before, I've been through all this before. I can relate."

"Is that all?" I asked suspiciously.

"For now." Dylan shrugged. "Anyway, I don't mind you owing me a few favors. You never know when I'll need to collect. See ya." And she left, closing the door behind her.

It was a little weird to have this new, nicer Dylan in my life. I wondered when she would change back. It made me think of my parents' "teen angst" comments. Maybe she was over the bad years, and I was the new Dylan? The thought horrified me, and I shuddered. But it was kind of right on track. I remember when Dylan turned thirteen, suddenly, there was a lot more fighting, more slamming doors, lots of crying, some bad grades. I seemed to be following the same pattern. And, if all stayed true to Dylan's path, it meant there would be two more hard years to come before my parents and I pulled out of it. It also meant it was likely that I'd have a boyfriend soon! That thought, at least, made me smile.

My mom and I kind of avoided each other the next morning, and she was at work when the Cupcakers and I got home from school on Friday to bake at our house. I was upset about missing out on all the fun for Saturday, so I hadn't really been able to break it to my friends yet. In other words, they had no idea I wasn't able to go on our Saturday outing.

"Oh, and I saw something really cute at Trudy's last weekend. We should go there tomorrow too!" said Mia. Trudy's was this cheap and trendy store at the mall, good for dressy stuff and accessories.

"Great," I said, fake-happy. Mental note: Go to Trudy's sometime.

We dumped our stuff in the back hall and began setting up for the baking session. Katie had brought some licorice whips to make whiskers for the cat cupcakes, and we had little candy wafers for the puppies' ears. We also had to bake the six dozen cupcakes for the barbecue, and Mona's minis.

We got to work doing an assembly line for the cupcake batter first. We'd be baking thirteen dozen cupcakes in all, so it wasn't a small job. Katie measured the dry ingredients while Emma did the wet ones. I put the paper wrappers into the muffin pans (we only had four of them, and two ovens, so we'd have to do everything a few times). Pretty soon, we were ladling the batter into the cupcake papers and putting them all in the oven. We couldn't wash any dishes yet since we had another round to go, so Emma suggested Mia and I go tackle my clothes.

"But . . . ," I began to protest.

"You don't have to tell me twice!" said Mia, starting out to the stairs.

"Go on," said Emma. "Remember? I promised we'd help you. This is us helping you!" She smiled, and I followed Mia out with a "Thank you!" over my shoulder.

Upstairs, Mia was already in my room. "Let's start with bottoms," she declared. "They're like the protein in a meal. You can build everything else around them. What do you have that fits?"

I pulled out the remaining pair of pants and a pair of shorts, plus the capris from my mom, and a long, green, stretchy tank dress.

"Do workout clothes count?" I asked. I knew Mia hated it when people wore workout clothes in public, so I was just teasing her.

"No!" Mia shuddered. "They're for *working out!* For that, you're on your own."

I watched as she neatly laid out each item around the room. "Okay, tops!" she ordered, and I took out a tank top, a very worn-in denim button-down shirt, and gestured to the turquoise T-shirt I was wearing again.

"Okay, love the T-shirt. Seen way too much of it lately. But the cut and size are great on you. Grab a paper and pen. We're going to do twenty looks with as few items as possible, and we're going to make a list of a couple of things you need to fill in." She started calling out ideas, and I jotted them down as fast as my pen could write.

Here was Mia's side of the conversation: "Two more of that exact T-shirt, different colors. They're on sale at Big Blue right now for fourteen dollars and ninety-nine cents. One more tank in white, I think; also cheap. We can layer a colored T-shirt over this dress; that's one look. Write it down. Then the tank over another colored T-shirt, with white jeans. Cute! Do you have a good belt that fits? What about a scarf we could use as a belt? Even better. Now where's that white denim mini you had on at the beach? Oh, it's not yours. Okay, put that on the list. Icon is selling them—yes, I know you hate Icon—for nineteen dollars, just this weekend. How do I know all this? I follow the sales online, chica! Now how about the capris? No, they do not make you look like a scarecrow, you're just wearing the wrong shoes with them! What do you have in a wedge? Nothing? What do you mean you don't want to look taller? I'd *kill* to be as tall as you. Work what you've got, girl!"

I wished Dylan were here to see this. She'd be in her element. Naturally, she and Mia adored each other. I couldn't wait to show Dylan what Mia came up with. Already there were three cute looks on my list, none of which I would have thought of myself.

My pen moved furiously over the page, and after coming up with each basic look, Mia insisted on completing them with footwear, accessories, and jewelry. She had such a good eye, it was incredible. Time flew, and pretty soon I had a list a whole page long that detailed things I needed to buy or scrounge from Dylan and my mom.

"Mia, this is going to cost a fortune!" I cried.

She came and looked at the list over my shoulder. "Okay, the T-shirts, the tank, the white denim skirt—that's up to about sixty or seventy dollars. You need a very simple pair of white cotton pants; I bet we could get those for around twenty or twenty-five dollars. And the other stuff—shoes, belts, scarves, maybe a dress or two?"

Mia looked at me carefully. "With your flowing red hair and the pretty freckles, you could pull off a bit of a soft, hippie-sundress look if you wanted. Sandals. Beads." She tipped her head sideways and studied me. "Or maybe a fifties thing—belted waist, full skirt . . . Hmm. Well, we'll see what the stores hold tomorrow."

I cringed. I had to tell the truth. "Mia . . . I'm . . . I don't think I can go tomorrow. I wanted to tell you all day. My mom is making me go to my grandma's out in the country."

Mia's face fell. "What? Seriously? I was looking forward to finding you just the right thing for the barbecue on Sunday. Are you really gone for the whole day? Wait, you can't even come to the bake sale?"

I shook my head sadly. "Not unless I get a last-minute reprieve, but it doesn't look good." I sighed. "I'm so sorry to let you down."

"Me? Don't be silly. I just feel bad for you. You were excited to do this, weren't you?"

I nodded. "Yeah."

"Can you just . . . I don't know, take a rain check?"

"I don't think so. My mom's been pretty nice lately, except for this. Now we're in a fight. I feel bad. I think I have to go."

Mia sighed. "Okay. I get it. I sure know what it's like to have plans in two places." Since Mia's parents got divorced, she splits her time between their two homes—one in the city and one here.

"Thanks. If anything changes, you'll be the first to know."

Mia brightened. "I might have something I can lend you for the barbecue, anyway. I'll look."

"Great. Thanks. I think I'd better clean this up. You are so awesome at all this. I never would have thought of any of the things you came up with. Thank you so much!"

Mia grinned. "For me, it's a blast. I can't see why anyone would own anything they wouldn't use all the time, in many different ways, you know? It's kind of like solving a math equation, turning things around until they fit, chucking them if they don't."

I laughed. "You know I can relate to that! So should I just get rid of everything else?"

Mia nodded. "Yup. Just a little piece of advice, though: Make sure you check with your mom before you put anything that might be special in the giveaway pile. You know how funny moms can be."

"Hmm. Good point. I will," I agreed.

Mia helped me pull out everything I wasn't keeping, and everything else (which was about six or so items) went back into my drawers and closets. I felt so light and carefree with all those empty drawers and hangers. I realized I'd become kind of a slacker about weeding things out. There was so much stuff I hadn't worn in years.

"People could really use this stuff too!" said Mia. "It's too small for you, but it's still nice."

I held up an Irish sweater that my grandma had given to me. "Chuck it?"

Mia gasped. "No! That's an heirloom. Don't throw that away!"

I refolded it and put it on my bed. "I'll see what my mom says. Honestly, I never really wore it. It was always so scratchy."

Just then, Emma and Katie came trudging up the stairs.

"We're done with the first batch of cupcakes. The second round is in," said Emma.

"Holy closet explosion!" cried Katie.

"It looks worse than it is," I protested. "We just need to get this stuff into some bags."

"We can help you," offered Katie.

I got the bags, and we packed them up, trundled

them down the stairs to join the other two bags at the back door, and then turned back to the baking. Katie had made a basic vanilla frosting while we were working upstairs, and now it was time to start tinting and laying out the supplies for the decorating.

I broke the news to Emma and Katie about having to go to my grandma's, and they were bummed too, but they understood. Most kids are used to being bossed around by their parents for no good reason, I guess.

We decorated the cupcakes for the bake sale, and they came out so cute that I wished I could be there to see them sell tomorrow. I knew they'd fly off the platter like hotcakes. We sealed up the other plain cupcakes and the extra frosting in big plastic tubs to be ready to decorate first thing Sunday morning.

By the time my parents and Dylan got home, you would never have known how much had been accomplished at our house that day. I wished every day could be like that.

CHAPTER 9

Puff

ℐ had avoided speaking to my mom for most of the night. I don't think she even noticed, but the small act of rebellion made me feel better, at least.

At nine thirty, I got into bed and as usual, she came upstairs to say good night to me. Then she spied the Irish sweater on my desk.

"Oh, Lexi. The Irish sweater from Grandma." She held it up and shook it out a little. "So pretty. Are you giving it away?"

"Hmm," I said. I was lying on my back, staring at the ceiling. I was sure she was going to tell me I had to keep it. Technically, it still fit.

"Did you . . . ever wear it?"

"Nope," I said.

"Why not?" She refolded it and put it back on the desk.

I sighed. "Too scratchy," I said.

She smiled. "You know it was mine when I was a girl?"

"I guess," I said. I was kind of annoyed she was being all chummy, and now I was already picturing myself having to put it back in my pristine, empty closet.

She dropped her voice to a whisper. "Did you know I hated it?"

I looked over at her in surprise. This wasn't going the way I had expected.

"Why?" I asked. Despite my annoyance, I was intrigued.

"Too scratchy!" she said, laughing. "But my mom wouldn't let me get rid of it, because it was a gift from her mom! So she hung on to it for all these years and then passed it along to you when it turned up in an attic cleanout. She and I had one of the biggest fights of our life over this sweater."

"Really?" It was impossible for me to picture my mom and my grandma fighting. I propped myself up on an elbow. She'd hooked me back into talking to her now, darn it!

My mom nodded. "We were going to visit my

grandmother, and I didn't want to go, because there was a dance at school I'd have to miss. And on top of it, my mom was making me wear that sweater so my grandma would be pleased to see me in it. I was furious. We screamed and yelled and slammed doors. . . ."

"How old were you?" I asked.

My mom tipped her head to the side. "About thirteen," she said.

"So what happened?" I asked. "Did you get out of it?"

My mom shook her head. "Nope. I had to go. And I had to wear the sweater." She reached over and gave it a pat. "And I swore then that I would never make plans for my kids without checking with them first."

I bolted upright, and my jaw dropped. "But you did!" I accused.

My mom sighed. "I know. I guess when you're a kid, you don't realize that adults have feelings too. My mom must've had a reason for us to go see my grandma. Maybe she felt she'd been neglecting her, or maybe she suddenly seemed old."

"Is that why you're making us go tomorrow?" I asked.

"Pretty much," said my mom. "But you know

what I realized? I checked with Dylan and not with you. I learned my lesson with Dylan a couple of years ago. It hit me all at once that she was an independent person, capable of making her own plans and sticking to a schedule. Your father and I raised you girls to be that way, and it's a good thing! So after one too many times of assuming she was still a little kid whose schedule I controlled, I backed off and started *asking* rather than *telling* her what our plans were—or most of them, anyway. Some things are still commands."

"Like tomorrow?" I said, grumpy again.

"No, not like tomorrow," said my mom. "I made a mistake. I was still thinking of you as a little kid, without concrete plans of your own, and I was wrong. I should have checked with you. So you're off the hook. You can go with your friends and do the things you need to tomorrow."

"Wait, really?" I asked. Excitement washed over me with the realization that I was now free tomorrow. It seemed too good to be true. "Are you sure?"

She nodded, and I hopped out of bed and hugged her. "Thank you, Mom! Thank you so much!"

She patted my back. "Maybe you'd make Grandpa Jim a birthday card in the morning? I'll explain you had some work commitments and couldn't make it."

"Thanks, Mom. I will. This is great news! I need to text my friends."

She laughed. "Okay. Just keep me posted on your schedule in the future, and I'll do the same. It will definitely help us in navigating at least *some* of the teen angst, okay?"

"Okay!"

The Cupcakers came over first thing the next morning, and we got to work decorating the puppy and kitten cupcakes. They turned out so well that we took pictures of them to put on our website, figuring they would be cute for birthday parties.

Emma had already delivered the minis to Mona before she came over, so we packed the bake sale cupcakes into our carriers, and my mom drove us to the animal shelter before she left with Dylan and my dad for Grandma's.

The animal shelter was in a small strip mall— a pretty nice new one, actually—and it had an awning that overhung the front of the shelter, so they'd set up the bake sale tables under there, right in front of the clinic doors. There weren't many other stores built in the mall yet—just a coffee store and a hardware store, but those two places were plenty busy on a Saturday morning, so there was a lot of foot traffic for the bake sale.

The organizers all squealed with delight when we unpacked our cupcakes. I had remembered to bring our business cards that listed our names and the website, so I placed those in a small pile next to the disposable platter that held our cupcakes. Some of the grown-ups were so impressed, they took pictures, and I handed out business cards to everyone there. You never know where your next opportunity could come from!

Mia wanted to go inside to see say hi to her vet, and since we had arranged to call Mrs. Brown when we were ready for a ride home, we all agreed. Inside, we quickly found Dr. Palmer, who was supernice and friendly, and very grateful to have what he called "professional baked goods" for the bake sale.

"Have you seen our kittens?" he asked. "Know anyone looking for one?"

"Ooh, I love kittens!" squealed Katie. "But my mom's allergic."

He waved us in, and we followed him down a little hallway.

"Too bad," said Dr. Palmer. "Cats make great

pets. Here we are!" He led us into a little tiled-floor room, and there were about eight kittens roaming around, climbing a carpeted pole, batting a ball around, sleeping curled up together in a smush of kitten fur in a basket. It was like a Richard Scarry book I used to read when I was little, with all the animals doing different activities all over the page.

I dropped to my knees. "Oh my gosh, they are so cute!" I cried. "Here, kitty, kitty, kitty."

One by one, my friends crouched down, and we all started trying to attract the kittens. Dr. Palmer laughed. "You might be here awhile. They love people. And it's hard to leave once you start."

"Look at me!" cried Emma. She's a major animal lover. Two kittens were tentatively climbing across her lap, testing with their little paws before they took another step up her leg.

"Can we just pick them up?" I asked.

Dr. Palmer nodded. "Sure. They've all had their shots, so they're good to go. The more they're handled at this age, the better. You girls are old enough that I don't have to warn you to be gentle. I'll leave you here for a bit while I see a patient. If you're going to go, just make sure none of them escape before you close the door."

"Thanks!" we called.

There was this one little inquisitive gray fluff ball that was just so adorable. I scooched across the floor and picked it up. It fit in the palm of my hand, and it was so warm and soft.

"Oooh, you are too cute!" I said, scratching behind its little ears. It began to purr really loudly, like a motor, and I laughed. It nestled down in the crook of my folded leg and fell asleep almost instantly. "I love this little guy," I said.

"You should adopt him," said Emma.

"As if!" I laughed. "Can you imagine my parents allowing a pet in the house?"

Emma laughed now. "Actually, probably not. Mia, can you take one?"

Mia shook her head. "Not with the dogs. It wouldn't be fair. Why can't you?"

"Too many mouths to feed already," said Emma a little sadly. "I wouldn't even ask." Emma's family has four kids, and they have a dog.

We played a little longer, and in my mind I named the little guy Puff, because he was like a puff of smoke. Finally, it was time to go. I hated to leave Puff, even though we'd only known each other for half an hour. It just felt so good to have that cozy little squish ball snuggled against my leg.

"Bye, baby," I whispered into his fur. He smelled

like warm wool, like a baby lamb (or an Irish sweater!).

"Let's go, Alexis," said Mia from outside the door.

Reluctantly, I finally stood and left the room. In the waiting area, we said good-bye to Dr. Palmer. When we counted everything up, we realized our cupcakes were already more than half sold! It had been a great morning. Katie called her mom for a ride to the mall, and while we waited, Mia noticed that the empty store next to the shelter was a temporary thrift shop.

"Hey, lucky coincidence! Let's see what they have! Do you have your list, Lexi—Alexis?" she asked.

I nodded and patted my tote bag. I had some of my savings, plus forty dollars from my grandma, and fifty from my parents for new clothes. I was feeling very flush with cash.

Inside there were folding tables with signs above them that said things like GIRLS, SIZE 6–12 or WOMEN'S SHOES. It was kind of depressing from a merchandising perspective, but Mia wasn't fazed by it in the least. That girl is all about the clothes!

"Come!" she said, gesturing me toward the women's shoes area. There were a few people in there, and the women's shoes table backed up to the teen girls' shoe area, probably because of the size overlap. Mia was like a laser beam, focused on my list (one pair of wedges, one pair of strappy sandals, Keds or similar flat casual shoes). Her shopping on my behalf allowed me to look around and absorb the scene.

"Try these," she said, turning to me with a pair of copper-colored flat sandals and a pair of wedges in navy.

"Umm, okay!" I said, and I slid off my shoes and tried the wedges. They made me quite a bit taller—the heel was about two inches high—but they were comfy.

"How much?" I asked, feeling price sensitive after watching a teenager and her mom argue about the price of something.

"Fourteen," said Mia. "But they're brand-new. The soles aren't even scuffed. They're perfect with your capris and also the long dress."

"I think I'll get these," I said of the wedges. I tried the sandals on, but the straps cut into my ankles too much, and I knew I'd have instant blisters.

While I was paying at the checkout, a woman came in laden with shopping bags that looked just like the ones I'd left at home.

"Donations?" asked the clerk. When the lady nodded, he pointed her to a far corner of the store.

"Oh!" I said. "You take donations?"

"Yup. Weekends all day, weekdays after four p.m. Need to be clean and in good condition. We can give you a charity receipt for the write-off." He handed me my change and put my wedges in a plastic grocery bag.

"Thanks! I think I'll be back with some donations then, very soon."

"Great. Thanks for shopping here!"

Katie poked her head into the doorway of the store. "My mom's here, guys!"

I made a mental note to ask my mom to help me bring my bags here, and then, without time for a final visit to Puff, we left for the mall.

CHAPTER 10

Fashion Equation

At the mall, Mia is like a military general. She can really lead a shopping expedition. There was no time to waste.

Mia's master plan was that we'd work around a palette of white and navy, with "pops of color" in accessories or secondary pieces. I liked the mathematical simplicity of it all. We took a standard equation: navy and white, and worked in variables, like turquoise and pink. So if the shoes were navy wedges, and the pants were white capris, that meant I could play around with my top, color-wise; it could be any color since the other two were my neutrals. It made perfect sense to me when she explained it like that.

We hit Big Blue first, since we knew they had what I needed. I snapped up two T-shirts (a white and a navy, under Mia's direction) just like my mom's turquoise one, on sale just as Mia had said they'd be. At the checkout, we scored a white tank top for eight dollars in a promotional bin, and Mia was thrilled.

"Icon, next," she said as I paid.

I sighed heavily. Icon is not a store I like.

"Emma and I are going to the bathing suit store," said Katie. "Want to just meet us there, after?"

"Great," we agreed, even though I didn't mean it. I wished I didn't have to go to Icon. I watched Katie and Emma longingly as they disappeared around the corner.

I cannot stand Icon because the music is loud, the store is dark so you can hardly see anything, and they use so much cologne or something that it reeks. It's sensory overload. Mia thinks it's fun because it's "the ultimate shopping experience." I guess it's just not my kind of experience.

She asked a salesperson where the denim mini-skirts were, and he pointed us to the far side of the store. Briskly, Mia strode across and snapped hangers across the pole until she reached my size. "I think you should get the dark blue denim rather than the white, but try both!" she yelled over the music as she handed me the hangers. "I'm going to look for a couple of other ideas. I'll meet you in the fitting room line."

Another thing I hate about Icon is that the line for the fitting rooms takes forever. They only have three rooms, and from a business perspective, I think they do it so that it makes the store seem really popular. (The same way they make you line up outside behind a velvet rope to be let in on days when they get new shipments.) I think the whole thing is kind of phony, but I supposed if you're not on to them, you might fall for it and think the store is supercool. I just think they need more fitting rooms.

The line moved rather quickly today, and then it stalled. I had snaked into the part of the fitting room where it was still pretty dark but not as loud. I was leaning against a wall, waiting for my turn, when I heard angry voices coming from one of the rooms.

"But I *need* it! It's exactly perfect for the barbecue!" whined a girl.

A grown-up's voice was speaking sternly back, but I couldn't hear what the person was saying. It must've been a girl and her mom fighting. I cringed, imagining how bad things would have to be between me and my mom before we'd fight in public.

"You are so *mean!*" the girl's voice cried, and her fitting room door banged open, causing everyone to turn and look.

It was Olivia Allen, being followed out by her visibly angry mother.

I ducked back a little into the shadows so she wouldn't see me, but I couldn't help staring as Olivia stepped onto a little podium in front of the three-way mirror. She was wearing a very skimpy, fitted, black tank dress. She primped and posed in front of the mirror while her mother stood behind her, her arms folded across her chest and her mouth firmly pressed into a line.

"It's inappropriate," her mother declared.

"I don't care! I'm getting it!" said Olivia, and she flounced off the podium.

Right then, they called "Next," and it was me. Quickly, I darted into a fitting room without Olivia noticing me.

"Phew!" I said to myself once I was safely inside. But then I heard Mia.

"Alexis! Alexis!" she was outside calling my name. "Alexis Beck-er!" she singsonged.

Ugh!

"Shh!" I opened my door quickly and grabbed her, dragging her inside.

"What's up?" Mia laughed. "Is someone after us?"

"Maybe," I said. "Olivia Allen is in here."

"Oh," said Mia in a "who cares?" kind of voice. They were friends for a little while but Olivia treated Mia really badly so now Mia avoids her.

"She and her mom were fighting," I said darkly.

Mia shrugged. "Well, what else is new? Here, I got these for you to try. I'll wait outside. Do the denim mini first, though. I know that will be a keeper."

Mia ducked out since the fitting rooms are tiny. I yanked off my pants and pulled on the mini. Just for fun, I pulled out the wedges from the bag and stuck them on too, then I trotted out to the viewing podium. (Ugh. I hate everyone looking at me.)

Mia whistled. "Woo-hoo! Now those are a pair of legs!"

I blushed, which luckily no one could see in the dark, and turned this way and that kind of quickly, looking but wanting to get it over with.

An older lady leaned over and said to me, "That looks lovely, dear. If I had your legs, it'd be all I'd wear!"

I smiled and thanked her, still feeling a little self-conscious. Like, why would I play up these darn limbs that are giving me so much trouble right now? Growing too long, out of proportion, painful, keeping me up at night . . .

"Work it, girl!" said Mia. "You are getting that. And with tights and boots, you can wear it all year-round. Next!"

I climbed down from the podium and walked straight into Olivia, who was coming out of her fitting room and measured now a full head shorter than me since I was in heels. She looked up.

"OMG, Alexis, you're a giant all of a sudden! You're going to tower over all the boys in those things!" And she turned and walked off while my jaw was still hanging open.

I knew she was just being mean, and as I've said, I've been through this before with her. As her mother passed by, she said, "I apologize for my daughter. She's acting like a spoiled brat today." And she walked on.

Now my jaw was hanging even lower. Imagine my mom having to apologize for my behavior! I continued to my fitting room and saw they'd left theirs a mess, with discarded clothes draped all over everything and in a pile on the bench. Gross. What a pair those two were.

At that point, I'd lost my enthusiasm for

shopping, barbecue outfit or not. I halfheartedly tried on a couple of the things Mia had pulled, but I wasn't that into them. I was happy with the skirt for nineteen dollars, and I wanted to get out of Icon.

Mia was a little disappointed, but she understood as I handed all my rejects back to the fitting room clerk (all neatly on their hangers, thank you very much!).

I paid for my denim miniskirt, and we headed out to find the other two Cupcakers. Outside, I gasped in relief, even though my ears rang like I'd just been at a loud concert. Turning, we spied Olivia and her mom still fighting. I guess they hadn't bought anything because they weren't holding any bags. I tried to feel sorry for Olivia, but I couldn't. There was no choice but to pass by them. Otherwise, we'd have to do a whole circuit of the upper level to get to the bathing suit store. I was hoping we'd go by unnoticed, but right as we reached them, Olivia's mom said, "Go on!" and Olivia turned to me.

"Alexis, I'm sorry I was rude to you in there. I was mad at my mom, and I took it out on you. The skirt and the shoes looked very pretty on you."

Her mother stood, nodding, over her shoulder.

"Uh . . . I . . . ," I stammered, shocked.

"Thanks, Olivia," said Mia, and she grabbed my arm to keep my feet moving.

"Thanks," I sputtered as Mia dragged me away.

"That girl is too much," said Mia, once we were a few stores away.

"I know. She really knows how to get to me," I said.

"You do realize that she goes after your best assets, don't you?" Mia asked.

"What do you mean?"

"Well, your cute freckles, your superlong legs—those are some of the great things about you. It's like a joke that she'd even try to be negative, since they're such obvious pluses!"

"Really?" I was surprised by this analysis.

Mia nodded. "Very typical of mean-girl behavior. I've read up on it."

"Yeah," I agreed. "Well, it still hurts. I know my legs are freakishly long."

"Trust me. There's nothing freakish about them. They're an asset," said Mia. "And I know these things."

We reached the bathing suit store and found Katie and Emma finishing up. They'd been laughing their heads off, trying on inappropriate bathing suits, and I was sad to have missed it. Plus, I needed a new suit myself.

"I'll be quick," I said.

Mia picked a couple of one pieces for me to try, and I quickly settled on a navy suit with white trim.

"Very sharp." Mia nodded. "You could wear the white tank over it, and the denim skirt."

"Maybe. Just not to the beach." I laughed. "I wouldn't want to be overdressed again."

"With some beads, you could definitely wear it tomorrow. Let's try Trudy's, and then maybe I'll let you off the hook for the day."

At Trudy's, some of the stuff was truly off the wall. Wild prints, tight, short, tacky. Not much I'd wear, though Mia unearthed a navy-and-gold rope belt, as well as a white chiffon scarf that was pretty and a pair of "gold" five-dollar hoop earrings. She made me get them, but I refused to try on anything else.

We decided to go for a smoothie and call Mia's mom for a ride home. I appreciated all the work Mia had put into my wardrobe, so I insisted she let me treat her to a smoothie.

As we sat waiting for Mia's mom to text that she was here, everyone talked about what they'd wear tomorrow. The barbecue was a twelve-thirty lunch, so it wouldn't be too dressy—more of a daytime look, said Mia.

"The boys are just going to wear shorts and polo shirts. They're so lucky," said Katie. "It's so easy for them."

"You'd be surprised," said Emma wisely. "There's a lot of trying on before they're happy with how they look."

"Really?" I asked. I couldn't picture it.

She nodded. "Some shirts pull in the wrong places, some are too tight in the neck, some are bad colors—like if their moms pick them out, they might be pink or purple or something. Sometimes the boys worry that they look fat, or overdressed or underdressed. It's all kind of the same as us."

"I simply do not believe it," I said.

Emma laughed. "Okay! One day, you'll have sons, and you'll know I was right."

"And they'll be your nephews!" teased Katie.

"I hope so!" said Emma, which was nice.

Since we'd need to be there by noon with the cupcakes, we agreed we'd meet up at my house at ten thirty to do the decorating, and then we'd change, and my mom would drive us over together.

Mrs. Velaz texted to say she was outside, and we all went out to meet her for rides home.

I was happy with my purchases and resolved in my mind to not be like Olivia Allen. I hadn't found the perfect thing to wear, but I had great friends who had tried to help me, and a mom and sister who'd also made a big effort to make me look good. The perfect dress would have only been the icing on the cake.

CHAPTER 11

Party!

"Lexi? Honey? We're home!" my mom called up the stairs. It was four o'clock. "Ugh! I'm tripping over all these bags in the back hall, honey!"

I darted downstairs. "Hi, Mom. Sorry! How was it?"

Dylan followed her in, her arms laden with shopping bags. "Awesome!" she crowed, putting everything on the kitchen table. "Grandma went wild because I hadn't been there in so long."

"You lucky duck! Show me everything!"

"Alexis, can we move these bags of old clothes to the basement, maybe?" My mom was looking harassed.

"Oh, Mom! I have a genius plan. You know the animal shelter that we went to this morning?

There's a thrift shop next door, and we can donate the stuff there. They'll even give us a receipt for your taxes."

"Wonderful!" said my mom. "How soon can we go?"

"Seriously? We could go now!"

"Okay, let me make a quick cup of coffee, and then I'll run you over."

"Thanks!"

Dylan gave me a tour of everything she'd gotten. There was some really pretty stuff, and I was happy for her, especially because she likes clothes way more than I do. She wanted to see what I'd gotten, and I went to get it and explained all about the white-and-navy-palette concept.

"Mia is so chic," said Dylan, shaking her head admiringly. "It's genetic."

Dylan worships Mia's mom. She wants to be her intern this summer, if possible, even if it's only a volunteer job.

"Ready?" asked my mom, taking one last quick gulp of coffee. "Let's go!"

We loaded the car with Dylan's help and then drove over to the shelter. The bake sale had closed up for the day, and the thrift shop was getting ready to close too. The same guy was there from this morning, and he was happy I'd come back with donations. I put the bags in the corner, and while he made up the receipt with my mom, I looked at the teen girls' clothing table a little.

There was a pretty one-piece romper, believe it or not. I had to laugh, thinking of Dylan's failed romper experience. This one was a lightweight white linen, with tiny navy blue Xs embroidered onto it. It had short sleeves, and blue buttons all up the front and a little gathered waist. I held it up and turned it this way and that. It would actually be perfect to wear tomorrow with my new espadrilles. The price tag caught my eye: It was four dollars.

"Mom!" I called. She turned, and I held up the romper.

"Cute!" she called "Can you try it on?"

The guy directed me to a makeshift changing area (so different from Icon), and I quickly put on the romper and went out to show my mom.

"Oh, Alexis, it looks so pretty! Very fresh and summery. I bet it's comfortable, too."

I nodded. It felt great. "I'm going to get it," I said.

"My treat," said my mom, and I thanked her and went to change.

It was funny how quickly I'd gone from feeling

weird about thrift shopping to getting kind of into it. I mean, an entire party outfit for under twenty dollars? It gave me a whole new outlook on spending.

We paid, and as we were going out to the car, Dr. Palmer was coming out of the shelter carrying a huge poster board. He waved, recognizing me from this morning. "Thanks for the cupcakes!" he called. "Still don't want a kitten?" he joked with a grin. He taped the poster board onto the big plate-glass window of the shelter. It said, FREE KITTENS!

"Oh, Mom, they have the cutest kittens ever! We were playing with them all morning. They're awesome!"

"I remember getting a kitten when I was your age," she said.

"Buggsy?" I asked. I'd heard about him before. He'd died a year after Dylan was born.

She nodded. "It was so exciting, getting that little guy. I'll never forget it." She smiled, remembering. It was weird to think of Mom having a pet. Any time Dylan and I had asked—or begged, really—Mom and Dad had always said no. "We're not pet people," Dad always said. Too much work, too much responsibility.

We waved at Dr. Palmer and then drove home,

and I told her all about Puff and how sweet and warm he was.

"It's great to have a pet to tell your troubles to," she reminisced. "Some parenting experts strongly recommend it."

"I know, I know, but we're not pet people," I said. There was a pause when I expected her to agree with me, but she didn't. "Are we?"

My mom shrugged. "When you guys were little, it seemed unnecessary to have a pet. Maybe we could entertain the thought now that you're old enough to help out."

"Really? Can we ask Dad?"

"I'll talk to him about it and see what he says."

"Huh. That would be really cool." And I stared out the window the rest of the way home, day-dreaming about what it would be like to have my own cat.

Sunday was sunny and cool, with weather predictions for a gorgeous early summer day. The Cupcakers showed up right on time, and the first thing I said to them was, "Guess what? We might get a cat!"

"Oooh, get Puff!" exclaimed Katie.

I had to "manage my expectations" (as my mom was fond of saying), so I said, "Well, he might be gone by the time we decide what we're going to do. I mean, it might be next year by the time we get one."

Katie nodded sadly. "Oh well. I guess there're other fish in the sea. Or kittens at the shelter."

We created an assembly line in the kitchen, with me putting on the base coat of blue frosting (the ocean), Emma rolling the side of it in brown sugar (the sand), Mia placing the strip of Airheads taffy on top (the beach towel), and Katie carefully making any final adjustments. We'd put the umbrellas on when we got to the Drehers' house, since they wouldn't fit in out carrier otherwise.

"Oh, girls, these look adorable!" my mom exclaimed when she came into the kitchen.

"And I bet they taste great too!" said my dad, following her in.

We all laughed because my dad is a cupcake hound, and we never have any junk food in the house, so he's always begging cupcakes off of us.

"Here you go, Mr. Becker," said Katie, laughing as my dad pretended he was doing us a favor by sampling it. My mom rolled her eyes.

"Alexis, your dad and I have some news, and I think it's okay if your friends hear it." She was smiling, so it couldn't be bad, but I still felt nervous at the formality of it. Everyone kind of froze, and my mom gestured at my dad to tell me.

"What?" I asked.

He cleared his throat. "Alexis, you can get a cat."

"*What?*" I whooped. All my friends cheered and carried on, hearing the news. "What made you decide?" I asked.

My dad grinned. "The cupcake."

"No, seriously," I pressed.

My mom stepped in, "Your father and I think you've shown a lot of responsibility lately, and we think it's time you got some recognition in the family for it."

"Wow! What about Dylan?" I asked.

"We already discussed it with her, and she is all for it," said my dad.

"She's angling for a used car to recognize *her* responsibility," said my mom wryly.

My friends and I laughed, and then the Cupcakers began hugging me and jumping up and down.

"When can we go get Puff?" I asked my parents. "I hope he's still there!"

My dad looked at his watch. "I don't think we should rush it. How about after the barbecue? You girls can come with us, if you'd like. I'll call Dr.

Palmer and let him know we'll be coming over."

We cheered and hurried to finish the cupcakes and then head upstairs to change.

"Mia, guess what? I found something when I went back to the shelter thrift shop! Wait till you see!"

I ducked into the bathroom to put on the romper, and when I came back Mia freaked out.

"OMG! It looks like a designer outfit you paid hundreds of dollars for! Oh, Alexis, it's great! What about if you try it with the new belt?"

I hadn't thought of that, and when I put it on, Mia stood back and put her palms together like she was praying, and then she delivered the verdict: "Divine."

We all laughed because our friend Mona at the bridal salon always says that, and now we use it as our highest compliment.

Dylan came in to see what the fuss was about, and she laughed and shook her head when she saw what I was wearing. "You have to have those legs to pull off a romper," she said.

"Thanks, I think," I said with a smile.

The others changed, and then it was time to go. "See you back here at three thirty!" called my dad.

❀

The party was a huge success. It turned out to be pretty casual, so I was glad I hadn't gotten superdressed up. After my trip to the beach, it wasn't a mistake I was eager to repeat. The Drehers had a pool, so it was only a matter of time before people went in. Mrs. Dreher had hired two lifeguards for the party, and lunch wasn't even over before George Martinez came out in his suit and jumped in.

"Are you coming in, Alexis?" asked Matt. It felt so formal to hear him call me that, I kind of winced.

"Yeah, sure," I said.

"Atta girl!" He laughed. "I knew I could count on you!"

I changed into my new suit, which was so much more comfortable than the old one because it actually fit.

The pool was pretty crowded and big, so it took a few seconds to find Matt and George. They were in the shallow end, tossing a Waboba ball around and didn't see me. They looked so cute splashing around. I whipped out my cell phone to snap a photo of them. They both suddenly looked my way, and I was nervous for a second, thinking they were going to be annoyed I was taking a photo. But instead they starting goofing around, really hamming it up for the camera. I could barely take the photo, I was laughing so hard. Suddenly, Matt said, "Hey, wait a minute!" He climbed out of the pool, soaking wet but as cute as ever. He gently took my phone out of my hands and put his arm around me.

"Let's take a selfie!" he said. "Say 'cheese'!" We both grinned, and he snapped the picture. He stared at it for a moment before handing the camera back to me. "Check it out. You're almost as tall as me now," he said. "We look good together." It took me a moment to find my voice, I was that shocked.

"Yeah, we do," I croaked.

Matt jumped back into the pool and yelled, "I want copies of all those photos!"

I walked away in a daze, without even going in for a swim. I had a photo of Matt with his arm around me. He liked me. He liked that I was tall, and freckled. And now I had proof.

I went to find the Cupcakers and to say good-bye to the Drehers. Mrs. Dreher handed me an envelope, and I thanked her. The cupcakes had been a huge hit, and three moms had asked for our contact info. (I don't put out business cards at private events, though I always wish I could. But I just think it's a little too pushy, you know? And sometimes our clients might like to pretend they made the cupcakes themselves.)

As we were leaving, Olivia Allen was just arriving.

"A little late, aren't you?" said Emma.

Olivia looked like she'd been crying. Her dress was way too dressy for daytime. "Are Bella and the other girls here?" she asked, craning her neck to see over our shoulders.

I shrugged. "I don't know. They were here earlier."

She looked at me like she was just noticing me. "Cute romper," she said. "Is it Chanel?"

I had to laugh at the idea of me affording an outfit from a designer like Chanel, let alone wearing it to a barbecue. "No," I said. "But thanks for the compliment." Our eyes met for a moment, and Olivia smiled.

"You're welcome. Bye." And she walked into the party alone.

The Cupcakers and I raised our eyebrows meaningfully at one another, and then we turned to go.

"Hey!" called a voice from behind us as we reached the gate. It was Matt.

We turned, and he jogged up, kind of out of breath. "I was looking for you guys everywhere."

"Well, here we are," said Emma, stating the obvious.

"Uh . . ." We all waited, and Matt grinned like an idiot. "Are you getting a ride home with Mom and Dad right now?"

"No, we're going to get Alexis's kitten, remember?" Emma said patiently.

"Oh," said Matt. He looked at me with a funny look on his face.

Before I knew what I was doing, I said, "Wanna come?"

"Sure! Thanks, Lexi!" He grinned like a maniac. "Let me tell George!" And he ran off without thinking twice about it.

"OMG, do you guys mind?" I said, suddenly ashamed of myself.

But my friends were all smiling at me.

"It's fine," said Emma. "It's not like he's a stranger. I mean, he calls you 'Lexi,' after all." She grinned, and I grinned back.

Puff was waiting for me when we got to the shelter that afternoon. Turns out my mom had called Dr. Palmer and caught him just as he was leaving yesterday, asking him to put a hold on Puff for twenty-four hours. Puff seemed to recognize me, I swear, and when I sat down with my legs crossed, he climbed right into the crook of my leg again and snuggled in and fell asleep, just like yesterday.

Everyone played with the other kittens while my dad did the paperwork with Dr. Palmer, and he got a cardboard carrier to bring Puff home in.

Driving home, Puff made peeping noises in the carrier that were so cute, I had to take him out. Then he got loose and climbed around the car, still mewing, until Matt caught him and snuggled him into his arms.

"He likes you," I said to Matt with a smile.

Matt looked down at Puff, and smiled too. "You think?"

I nodded. "For sure."

That night, I lay in my bed with Puff snuggled up against my long legs, purring in his sleep, and I could not have been happier. It had been a crazy couple of weeks with my body kind of going haywire. And my brain too, for that matter. I'd been scatterbrained, disorganized, messy, and cranky. My legs had ached as they'd grown, and I'd developed freckles on top of freckles. Besides, I'd failed a test, shopped at a thrift store, and been teen angsty with my mom. All out of character for me.

But I'd also found I had some of the best friends and the greatest family any girl could ever hope for. And I had an adorable new kitten that liked me, and maybe a boy who felt the same way. Who knows what was going to happen next? But everything was perfect right now. . . . Anything else would just be the icing on the cake—or the cupcake!

Want another sweet cupcake?
Here's a sneak peek
of the next book in the

CUPCAKE DIARIES

series:

Katie

starting
from scratch

Really, Mom?

So, Emily, what's new with you? How are things going at school?" my mom asked the girl sitting next to me.

"It's okay," Emily replied. "Everyone's been really nice, and I like all my teachers so far. But it's only been two days, so it's hard to tell."

Emily's dad, who was sitting next to my mom, smiled at her. "I think you're doing great."

I should probably remind you that Emily's dad, Jeff, is also a math teacher at the middle school that I go to. There I call him "Mr. Green," but I guess Emily just calls him "Dad." And Jeff, or Mr. Green or whatever you want to call him, happens to be dating my mom. It gets a little awkward sometimes to have your mom dating a teacher at school, but I'm dealing with it.

"Are you having trouble with the lock on your locker?" Mom asked Emily. Mom nodded toward me. "Katie had a hard time getting the hang of it. Once she even called me at work because she couldn't get it open."

I looked at my mom in disbelief. "Really, Mom? Did you have to tell everybody that?"

Maybe normally I would have just laughed at a comment about that (especially since Mom was right), but lately Mom was doing this thing with Emily, like sort of selling me out to get closer to her, that was starting to get annoying. Even more stuff happened during our dinner that night, at the Maple Grove Diner.

Mom changed the subject of my un-awesome lock-opening ability—but the conversation didn't get any better.

"Well, I'm glad everything is going smoothly for you," Mom said. "I remember when Katie and her best friend, Callie, just stopped being friends for no reason. Can you believe that? But, luckily, she made some new friends right away."

I. Could. Not. Believe. It. Mom was telling all my deep, dark secrets in front of Jeff and Emily.

"First of all, Callie stopped being *my* friend," I

said. "And anyway, why is this important? I have awesome friends now."

"That's exactly what I said," Mom protested.

"Well, I'm still friends with my elementary school friends," Emily said. "We even have some classes together."

That's when the waitress came to our table.

Finally, I thought. *We can stop talking about all my horrible school experiences and eat.*

Mom and Jeff both ordered turkey burgers and salads. Emily ordered a turkey club sandwich.

"Would you like fries with that?" the waitress asked.

"I'll have a salad, please," Emily said. "And a glass of water."

Then the waitress turned to me. "What would you like?"

Now, I like to think that ordering food at a restaurant is one of my skills. For example, if we go to Mariani's Italian Restaurant, I always order the eggplant parm because it's awesome there, but if we go to Torino's, it's too greasy so I get the ravioli, which they make by hand. And I always end up with the best food on the table. It's kind of an art. And whenever I recommend something, people always love it. Maybe I'll be a food critic when I get older. Imagine getting to eat in all the best restaurants and get paid for telling people what you did and didn't like. That would be pretty amazing.

Anyway, I know exactly what to order at the Maple Grove Diner. "I'll have the Reuben with cheese fries and a root beer, please," I said.

Now, for years Mom and I have eaten out a lot, just the two of us, so she is used to my mad food-ordering skills. But today she raised her eyebrows at me.

"Root beer?" she asked. "You know how I feel about soda. It's so bad for your teeth, not to mention your overall health."

My mom is a dentist, so of course I know how she feels about soda. Which made me think she was just saying that to impress Jeff or something.

"Mom, you know my food-to-beverage formula," I said.

Emily looked interested. "What is that?"

"Well, you know how some things just go together?" I asked. "Like, an ice-cold cola is awesome with Chinese food. But on the other hand, any kind of soda is gross with PB&J. The best drink for that is milk."

"What about . . . a tuna sandwich?" Emily asked.

"Iced tea," I said. "That would go great with a

turkey club, too, by the way. Or you can get lemonade."

"Dad, can I get an iced tea?" Emily asked Jeff.

"Well, I'd rather you didn't have caffeine this late," Jeff said. "But I think Katie's on to something. Maybe you can test her theory next time."

"I think it was very mature of you to order water, Emily," Mom said, and I tried my best not to groan out loud. We had hung out with Jeff and Emily kind of a lot over the past few weeks, and Mom was always saying stuff like that. Like she was comparing us, or something.

I was kind of mad at Mom for that comment, so I stayed quiet until the food came. My Reuben smelled amazing—it had corned beef, mustard, melted Swiss cheese, and sauerkraut. I know that might sound gross, but when you eat it all together, it's so good. And the cheese fries were covered with that gooey orange cheese. I ate one of those first.

"Whoops, Katie! You got some cheese on your shirt," Jeff said.

I looked down and saw a glob of orange cheese on my purple shirt. I grabbed a napkin and started scrubbing my shirt, but the cheese just left an orange streak. Mom rolled her eyes and gave a big sigh across the table.

Next to me, Emily was neatly cutting her salad into tiny pieces with a knife and fork. I realized that I had never seen her spill any food or anything like that. In fact, Emily is one of those all-over neat people. Her brown hair is always very neat and shiny, whereas my brown hair usually gets tangles in it by lunchtime every day. She wears white sneakers with no black smudges on them or anything, and I wear sneakers that I've doodled all over with colored pens. There's usually some kind of mud-like substance on them too.

Mom looked at Jeff. "Felix and Oscar," she said, and they both laughed.

"What's that supposed to mean?" I asked.

"It's from an old TV show about two roommates," Mom said. "One was really neat, and the other one was . . . messy."

"Let me guess. I'm the messy one?" I said, and Emily giggled next to me.

"It was a really funny show," Jeff said. I think he was trying not to make me feel bad.

"Very funny," Mom agreed, smiling at Jeff, and then they started holding hands at the table.

"Gross!" I mumbled, and then I bit into my Reuben. Mustard squirted out and landed on my jeans. Oh, well.

"Oh, I've been meaning to tell you," Jeff said, looking at my mom. "I'm not sure if I can go see that show with you next Saturday. Emily's mom has an unexpected business trip, so Em will be with me all weekend."

Emily's parents are divorced, just like mine. Except I never see my dad, and Emily sees Jeff every other weekend and some days during the week, too. It's hard to keep track of their schedules sometimes.

"Oh, that's a shame," Mom said. Then her eyes lit up. "Hey, it's a matinee, and we won't be back late. Why doesn't Emily hang out with Katie and her friends at their Cupcake Club meeting?"

I almost spit a mouthful of sauerkraut across the room.

"What?" I asked, with my mouth full.

"Well, Katie, you're old enough to babysit now, although this wouldn't exactly be babysitting," Mom said quickly. "And I'm sure you could use some help with your cupcakes."

I was speechless at first. Help? *Help?* At our Cupcake Club meetings, my friends Alexis, Emma, and Mia plan our schedules and go over our budget and come up with new cupcake ideas. We don't need help from anyone, let alone someone younger than we are. When we tried to add a new member, it didn't work out.

"I would love to help," Emily said a little shyly, and suddenly I felt badly for getting worked up. Yes, Mom thinking Emily was perfect was starting to get annoying, but Emily was pretty cool. And Emma's younger brother, Jake, comes to a lot of our meetings when Emma has to watch him, and Emily is kinda sorta like my younger sister, right?

"Fine," I said.

Mom smiled. "Perfect! Jeff and I can drop you off at Mia's for the meeting and then head into the city. I'll check with Mia's mom to make sure she can drive both of you back to our house."

"I just have to check with everybody first," I said, reaching for my phone.

"No texting during meals," Mom said, and I pulled my hand back and sighed. I had a club meeting tomorrow anyway, so I'd just mention it then.

Emily glanced at her dessert menu and then looked over at me. Her brown eyes sparkled under her perfect bangs. "What's the best dessert to go with a turkey club?" she asked.

I hadn't thought about dessert formulas before. This could get interesting.

"Hmm … Boston cream pie," I said. "Definitely."

"Dad, can I get Boston cream pie for dessert?" Emily asked.

Jeff laughed. "Sure, why not?"

So Emily got Boston cream pie for dessert, and I got rice pudding, to test and see if it would go well with a Reuben, which it did. Emily did not spill a drop of chocolate or whipped cream, but I managed to get a glob of pudding on my sneaker. And I didn't care one bit.

Something New

$\mathcal{K}$atie, I can't wait to try out that new thing you got," Emma said the next day. "Does it really make two-toned cupcakes?"

I nodded. "It's going to be awesome."

We were in my kitchen, having a Cupcake Club meeting. My friend Alexis was there too. The only member missing was my friend Mia. Her parents are divorced, and she spends every other weekend with her dad in Manhattan. Kind of like Emily, I guess. Anyway, it means that she can't be at every meeting. But all of us miss meetings sometimes, so it's not a big deal.

Alexis was scrolling down the screen of her new tablet. She had found this app that could track sales and expenses and stuff, and she was loving it.

"Katie, if you give me the receipt for that, the club could pay you back," she said. "You're always buying new equipment that we end up using."

I shrugged. "That's what allowance is for. I love buying this stuff."

"But in order to get a real sense of our profits, we have to keep track of our costs," Alexis argued. "Besides, it's only fair to you."

I wrinkled my nose, thinking. "I'm not sure if I have the receipt. I think I used it to throw out my gum."

"Well, next time, then," Alexis said, going back to her app.

I finished setting up the ingredients on my kitchen table: flour, sugar, eggs, cocoa powder, vanilla, baking soda, baking powder, milk, and butter.

"So, we need to make two batters," I said. "I thought we could start with vanilla and chocolate."

Then I picked up my latest baking tool: a two-toned cupcake insert. It's a white plastic thing that fits inside the cups in your cupcake pan. For each cup there's a plastic circle with another plastic circle in the middle. You pour a different flavor or color of batter into each circle, and then take out the insert before you bake them. The finished cupcake will have one color or flavor on the inside, and a different one on the outside.

"So why don't the batters run together when you take out the insert?" Emma wondered.

"I think because cupcake batter is so thick," I said. "Anyway, we'll see. That's what this test is about, right?"

We quickly made the two different batters—we're pretty much pros at making batter by now. Then I put the insert in the pan. It fits only three cups at a time. Alexis carefully poured chocolate batter into the center circle, and then I poured the vanilla batter into the outer circle.

"Here goes nothing," I said, lifting up the insert. Each cup now had a vanilla cupcake with a perfect circle of chocolate in the middle.

Emma clapped. "It works! Cool!"

I rinsed off the insert in the sink. "Let's do the whole pan."

When we finished filling the pan, I put the cupcakes in the oven. While they baked, we made a batch of chocolate frosting.

"Dibs!" I called out, taking the beaters off the hand mixer. Frosting was still stuck to it, and I licked it right off. "Mmm."

Emma laughed. "You remind me of Jake."

"Just Jake?" I asked. "Matt is always grabbing the beaters from me. Sam, too."

Emma shook her head. "I guess it's a good thing you don't have three brothers, then."

Emma mentioning Jake reminded me of Emily.

"I have something to ask you guys," I said. "I know we're baking next Saturday, but Mom wants me to watch Emily. Can I bring her to the meeting?"

"So your mom has another date with Mr. Green?" Alexis asked, wiggling her eyebrows.

I sighed. "It seems like she *always* has a date with Mr. Green lately." I lowered my voice. Mom was somewhere in the house, and I didn't necessarily want her to hear that. "They're going to some Broadway matinee or something."

"Sure, bring her," Alexis said. "She's practically our age, right? It's not like she's some annoying little kid or something. No offense, Emma."

"Believe me, I know how annoying Jake can be," she said.

The timer went off, and I took the cupcake pan out of the oven and put it on a cooling rack. We had to wait until the cupcakes cooled to frost them, or the frosting would just melt everywhere.

Alexis walked over to the pan. "You know, they look just like ordinary cupcakes," she said. "I mean, it's a cool idea, but how would people know they're special? It might not be worth the extra effort to make them."

I pulled a cupcake from the pan with my fingertips. "Let's see if it worked, first," I said. I took a knife and cut right through the cupcake. The chocolate cake center was perfect!

"That is really awesome," Emma said. "I bet people would love these, Alexis."

"Maybe we could cut one open and put it on the display," I suggested. "As an example."

Alexis nodded. "That could work. And our customers are always asking for something new. I'll add these to the order form."

"We should taste them first," I said. (I knew they were going to be great, but I never turn down a chance to taste a cupcake.)

The cupcakes were just about cool enough to frost, so we frosted them all. I poured glasses of milk for each of us (cupcakes and milk, the perfect pairing), and then we sat down and ate.

In my first bite, I got vanilla cake, chocolate cake, and chocolate frosting all in one. It was amazing.

"This is soooo good," I said, after washing down the bite with some milk. "Can you imagine all the other flavors we could do?"

"Red velvet and chocolate," Emma suggested.

"Or color combinations," Alexis said. "Pink and purple. Yellow and green. Kids would love that!"

We were quiet for a minute, enjoying our cupcakes and the sweet taste of success. Then Emma's blue eyes lit up.

"Oh, I almost forgot!" she said. "Principal LaCosta stopped me in the hall yesterday. She asked if the Cupcake Club would sell refreshments at the talent show."

"Oh, wow, that would be great," I said. "When is that, anyway?"

"Saturday the twentieth," Alexis said quickly.

"You are like a walking calendar," I said. "Is there anything you don't know?"

"Well, I don't know if this is such a good idea," Alexis said.

"Why not?" I asked.

"Yeah, it's perfect," Emma said. "We always sell a lot of cupcakes at school events."

Alexis started to twirl a strand of her wavy red hair. "I guess I meant that it's not a good day for me. I'm pretty sure I have a conflict."

"Well, that's okay," I said. "Emma and Mia and I could sell the cupcakes. As long as there's three, it's usually enough."

All About Alexis!

You have just finished reading a story about awesome Alexis. How well do you think you know her? Take this quiz and find out!

1. Alexis's last name is
   A. Taylor e
   B. Becker
   C. Brown k
   D. Valaz

2. Alexis's best friend is
   A. Mia
   B. Olivia
   C. Emma
   D. Katie

3. True or False: Alexis has straight blond hair.
   A. True
   B. False

4. Alexis has a sister named
   A. Dylan ✓
   B. Emily
   C. Ava
   D. Bella

5. Who is Alexis's crush?
   A. George
   B. Matt ✓
   C. Chris
   D. Jake

6. What is Alexis's best subject at school?
   A. Creative writing ✓
   B. Gym
   C. Spanish
   D. Math

7. What costume did Alexis wear to the pep rally parade?
   A. Gypsy ✗
   B. Ballerina
   C. Greek Goddess
   D. Angel

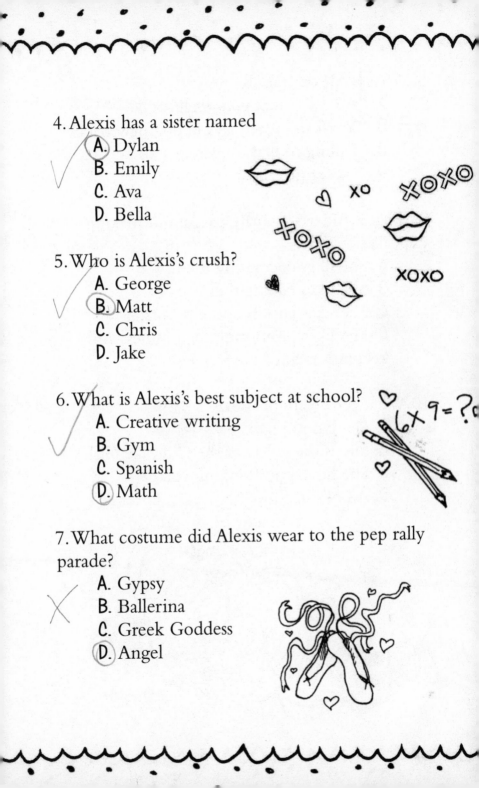

8. What is Alexis's family motto?
    A. "All's well that ends well."
    B. "You can't teach an old dog new tricks."
    C. "Failing to plan is planning to fail."
    D. "Never give up."

9. What is Alexis's favorite part about making cupcakes?
    A. She likes decorating them.
    B. She likes baking them.
    C. She likes choosing the flavors.
    D. She likes promoting the business and keeping track of the money.

10. What is true about Alexis?
    A. She has red hair
    B. She is the tallest of the Cupcake Girls
    C. She has a good singing voice
    D. All of the above

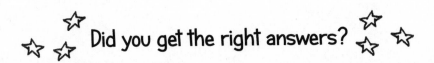 **Did you get the right answers?**

1.B 2.C 3.B 4.A 5.B 6.D 7.C 8.C 9.D 10.D

How did you do?
8-10 correct: Wow, you are officially one of Alexis's new BFFs!
6-7 correct: Not bad, but you need to pay a little more attention.
3-5 correct: Not so good. Alexis is a little disappointed.
0-2 correct: Oh, no! You need to try again and do better! Or else you'll be forced to eat lunch with Olivia Allen instead of the Cupcake Club!

Still Hungry?

There's always room for another Cupcake!

Katie and the Cupcake Cure
1

Mia in the Mix
2

Emma on Thin Icing
3

Alexis and the Perfect Recipe
4

Katie, Batter Up!
5

Mia's Baker's Dozen
6

Emma All Stirred Up!
7

Alexis Cool as a Cupcake
8

Katie and the Cupcake War
9

Mia's Boiling Point
10

Emma, Smile and Say "Cupcake!"
11

Want more

CUPCAKE DIARIES?

Visit **CupcakeDiariesBooks.com**
for the series trailer, excerpts, activities,
and everything you need for throwing
your own cupcake party!

Coco Simon always dreamed of opening a cupcake bakery but was afraid she would eat all of the profits. When she's not daydreaming about cupcakes, Coco edits children's books and has written close to one hundred books for children, tweens, and young adults, which is a lot less than the number of cupcakes she's eaten. Cupcake Diaries is the first time Coco has mixed her love of cupcakes with writing.